Katz's Uzi wa[...]
from his fingers

In the same instant the shadow of a descending hatchet crossed his face. Instinctively Katz raised his prosthetic arm in defense. Hatchet met steel in a bone-jarring collision as the blade of the Mongol's war weapon connected with the three-pronged hook on the end of the Phoenix Force pro's artificial arm.

Katz grunted as the pain vibrated all the way to his right shoulder, then charged beneath the uplifted arm holding the hatchet and stabbed out with his hook.

Pointed steel pierced the flesh of the Mongol's throat. Katz pushed farther, and blood spurted from the wound in a grim parody of a leaking faucet.

Mack Bolan's
PHOENIX FORCE

PHOENIX FORCE

Sea of Savages

Gar Wilson

A GOLD EAGLE BOOK FROM

TORONTO · NEW YORK · LONDON · PARIS
AMSTERDAM · STOCKHOLM · HAMBURG
ATHENS · MILAN · TOKYO · SYDNEY

First edition September 1985

ISBN 0-373-61319-9

Special thanks and acknowledgement to Paul Glen Neuman and
William Fieldhouse for their contributions to this work.

Copyright © 1985 by Worldwide Library.
Philippine copyright 1985. Australian copyright 1985.

All rights reserved. Except for use in any review, the
reproduction or utilization of this work in whole or in part
in any form by any electronic, mechanical or other means,
now known or hereafter invented, including xerography,
photocopying and recording, or in any information storage
or retrieval system, is forbidden without the permission
of the publisher, Worldwide Library, 225 Duncan Mill Road,
Don Mills, Ontario, Canada M3B 3K9.

All the characters in this book have no existence outside the
imagination of the author and have no relation whatsoever to
anyone bearing the same name or names. They are not even
distantly inspired by any individual known or unknown to the
author, and all the incidents are pure invention.

The Worldwide Library trademark consisting of the words
GOLD EAGLE is registered in the United States Patent
Office and in the Canada Trade Marks Office. The Gold Eagle
design trademark, the Executioner series design trademark,
the Phoenix Force design trademark, the globe design
trademark, and the Worldwide design trademark consisting
of the word WORLDWIDE in which the letter ''O'' is
represented by a depiction of a globe are trademarks
of Worldwide Library.

Printed in Canada

1

"Falling glass," the man observed, tapping his fingers against the barometer. "Pressure's dropping fast now. What do you think, Ferris? How long you figure we've got before the storm hits?"

Ferris checked the time on his wristwatch and smiled before replying. "That all depends, Mitchell, on which storm you're talking about."

"It's time, then?"

Ferris nodded. "Zero hour, my friend. The curtain just went up on the show, and we're the opening act."

Mitchell followed as Ferris moved confidently along the alleyway, the sensation of the steady rise and fall of the ship beneath their feet as natural to the naval veterans as walking across a concrete sidewalk would feel to the average man.

A minute later they stood on the upper deck of the ship, the sticky humidity of the open sea soaking through their uniforms almost immediately. The smell of salt hung in the air like the odor of stagnant water.

Ferris crossed and gripped the top of the bulwark. Already the clouds of the impending storm were playing their part in the evening's drama as if responding to cue. Overhead, the stars and the moon had been obliterated, cloaking the deck of the *Bruja del Mar* in a veil of murky black.

Flying the colors of the country of Colombia, the *Bruja del Mar* was something of an anomaly, a throwback to the sailing ships of a bygone age when crossing an ocean meant something more than batten down the hatches and full steam ahead.

Manned by a crew of twenty-five, the *Bruja del Mar* was part of an extensive maritime program sponsored by the Colombian government to ensure that the men of its navy served a mandatory three-month tour of duty upon a true full-rigged merchant ship. The *Bruja del Mar* was one of a fleet of six such vessels reserved for this training.

What separated the *Bruja del Mar* from her sister ships was the priceless cargo carried within her hold—a treasure trove of more than three hundred pre-Columbian gold artifacts and a vault full of precious emeralds. Part of a traveling extension of Bogotá's *Museo del Oro*, the floating museum's "Sweat of the Sun, Tears of the Moon" exhibition of gold objects and jewels was highlighted by a 1,759-carat emerald crystal that had captured the heart and imagination of everyone who had seen the gem on display.

Lieutenants Ferris and Mitchell were with the Office of Naval Intelligence and assigned to the ONI field office in Guam. When word came through that the Colombian government had contacted the American government and requested additional manpower for the security and protection of the *Bruja del Mar* during the Far Pacific portion of its voyage, Ferris and Mitchell were only too happy to volunteer for the prestigious assignment.

Ferris, Mitchell and a dozen men under their command boarded the Colombian ship when it stopped in Guam to take on supplies. They were to watchdog the floating museum during its visit to the Philippines, staying with the vessel until it safely reached Hong Kong.

Then a new detachment of ONI personnel would take over, sending Ferris and the rest back to Guam via a military transport flight.

Mitchell joined Ferris at the bulwark. "How do you want to work this?"

"Just like we planned. We want to have as many of the others as possible out of the way before our guests arrive."

"Good. I'll take the port side. You handle whatever you find starboard."

"And we'll meet at the bow," Ferris said as he turned away from the bulwark. "Keep your nose clean, Mitchell. Good hunting," he added.

And with that the men parted company, each going his designated way, thereby throwing into play the motions of a scheme that would secure their financial future for the rest of their lives.

"WHAT'S THE GOOD WORD, HOLMSTEAD?"

Startled by the unexpected appearance of his CO, the young E-3 jumped at the sound of Ferris's voice.

"Evening, sir," Holmstead managed to say, doing his best to diminish the fact that he had been caught off guard. "I'm afraid I didn't hear you approach."

"That's not too surprising," the ONI lieutenant admitted. "What with the wind and the waves and all, I would have been surprised if you *had* heard me. How's the night watch going?"

Holmstead shrugged. "Nothing much to report, sir." He brought his palms up empty-handed. "She's black as India ink tonight. We'll be catching a storm soon. You can feel it in the air."

Ferris leaned against the bulwark. "I think you're right, Holmstead. As a matter of—" Ferris stopped in midsentence and pointed across the water. ''What was that?''

Holmstead moved beside Ferris and stared out into the impenetrable darkness. ''What is it, sir?''

''A flash of light. I could swear I saw a flash of light.''

Holmstead leaned farther into the night, but could see nothing of the flashing light Ferris spoke of. ''I don't know, sir,'' Holmstead said, shaking his head. ''Whatever it was, it appears to be gone.''

''And so do you, Holmstead.''

''Sir?''

Lieutenant Ferris launched his attack, throwing his arm around Holmstead's head, pulling back, exposing the throat, then whipping the blade of the knife in his other hand in a vicious left-to-right slash.

Holmstead's eyes widened to pale saucers of pain as the flesh of his throat flapped open. A wet spray of blood washed across his chest; air leaked from the wound in a gurgling hiss. Holmstead struggled to scream, to call out for help, but there was no sound. He was dying. His final act of awareness told him he was being lifted from the deck and thrown overboard.

He was dead before his body hit the water.

Ferris watched as Holmstead's corpse sank beneath a wave, then continued on his way, slipping the knife into a sheath he wore at the back of his belt. Ferris felt his temples throb as a jolt of adrenaline rushed through his system. More than a year had passed since the last time he had killed, and this was the first time he had taken a life other than in the line of duty. Ferris found the natural high he was experiencing not unpleasant.

His next victim was even easier. A kid from Dayton named Barnett. No small talk with this one. It was over in a matter of seconds. Recognition registered on the kid's face an instant before the blade of the knife struck home, burrowing deep into Barnett's gut even as his knees buckled in death.

Ferris caught the sagging body as it fell, then heaved its deadweight overboard where it struck the water and vanished. Twice after that the ONI officer repeated his proved routine before reuniting with Mitchell at the bow of the ship.

"Well?" Ferris asked, noting that Mitchell's face had a sick, nervous look to it. With little prompting, Ferris reasoned, Mitchell could have washed the deck with his undigested supper. "Any trouble?"

"No." Mitchell faced the open sea, breathing deeply, drawing as much air into his lungs as he could. "I took out Dixon, Safire and Griffen."

"Good. By the time any of them are missed it will be too late to do anything about it. Counting the ones I got, that gives us a total of seven out of the way. Not a bad showing for a few minutes' work. What about the ladder?"

"Hanging over the side where it's supposed to be. What do you think?"

"Just checking. You look a little green around the gills."

"Because of Safire," Mitchell confessed. "The kid thrashed around like a chicken with its head cut off."

"The important thing is that he's out of the way." Ferris checked his watch. "It's 0100. Unless our friends ran into a snag we don't know about, they should be here any minute now."

"And we just stay put?"

"Until they've had time to identify us," Ferris advised. "Otherwise, we'd wind up like the rest, and that's the last thing we want. Can't take advantage of all that nice spendable money if we aren't alive to enjoy it.''

"Right," Mitchell agreed with an agitated laugh. "And with what we're gonna pull outta this deal, it would be a shame to have it any other way."

Ferris and Mitchell remained standing at the bow of the *Bruja del Mar* as they had been instructed to do. They waited, the seconds dragging to minutes and, because it suited his mood, Ferris passed the time by mentally counting from one to ten, over and over. He had repeated the process for a full five minutes when Mitchell quietly nudged him in the side and whispered, "They're here."

Ferris turned and confirmed that Mitchell was correct. Their co-stars for the second act of the evening's drama had indeed arrived.

Moving soundlessly across the deck of the ship, the newcomers looked more like wraiths than anything human. Dressed in form-fitting black uniforms, and with hoods over their heads so only their eyes were visible, they crept to the bow of the Colombian vessel until Ferris and Mitchell were surrounded.

Both Ferris and Mitchell glanced from left to right. Wind pushed at their backs as though forcing them into the arms of the shadowy figures they faced. Thunder cracked in the distance.

One of the black-clad warriors stepped forward and presented each American with an amulet attached to a gold chain. The symbol of a writhing three-headed snake dominated the talisman.

"Wear these." The man offering the amulets spoke with a heavy Oriental accent. "They are all that separates you from this world and the next."

Ferris and Mitchell accepted the snake-headed symbols and quickly put them on.

Mitchell gulped as the chain settled over his head and around his neck. "What...what should we do to help?"

The figure shrugged. "Try and stay out of our way."

And with that the leader of the assault team signaled to his companions and they were off, drifting back along the deck of the *Bruja del Mar* in search of prey.

"What do you think, Ferris?" Mitchell asked, fingering the amulet.

"The man gave us good advice," Ferris concluded. "We'll stay out of their way."

RAUL RENALDO SNAPPED HIS EYES OPEN and listened. For what, he was not sure. He had been sleeping peacefully, dreaming of the day when he would return to the arms of his beautiful wife, Maria.

Married only six short months when his orders came through for him to go to sea, Raul soon discovered that being separated from Maria was more than his overactive libido could endure. Of course, Maria sent him letters, but words on scented paper failed to quench the fires of desire burning in his breast. Raul longed to hold Maria in his arms, to taste the special flavor of her kisses, to enjoy the delights of her body until he succumbed, exhausted from the intoxicating pleasure of it all.

Until Raul returned to Colombia, though, the moments shared with Maria were only in his dreams. Each night she appeared to him, welcoming him to her bed, sharing herself with her man in a thousand different ways.

Tonight's dream had promised to be one of the best. Maria had called to him, begging him to take her, crying out for the delicious kind of satisfaction only he could supply. Raul had been eager and ready to satisfy Maria's urgent demands, but even as he reached to pull her into his arms, his beloved wife was gone, stolen by whatever it was that had roused him from his sleep.

Raul slipped his legs over the edge of his bunk and lowered his feet to the floor. Again he cocked his ear to catch any sound out of the ordinary, but all seemed as it should be. He contemplated lighting a lamp, but decided against it. Just because he was having trouble sleeping was no reason to wake anyone else.

Barefoot and in his underwear, Raul crossed to where the doorway to the crew's quarters opened onto the ship's main alleyway on B deck. He turned the door handle and created an opening wide enough for him to stick his head out for a look. The low-level lights of the corridor would enable him to see if all was well. His action brought him face-to-face with a pair of black-clad nightmares creeping toward him.

"*¡Joder!*" Raul exclaimed as the figure closer to him flicked both wrists in Raul's direction.

Raul screamed, staggering back into the crew's quarters, fingers clawing desperately to remove the shards of pointed steel jutting from his shoulder and neck. Blood spilled instantly from the wounds as three more of the deadly throwing stars struck home, etching Raul's bare chest in a constellation of death.

The young Colombian succeeded in flinging two of the barbs from his body before the poison that coated the last star to hit connected with his heart. Pink foam danced from Raul's lips as he dropped to the floor in a fit of convulsions, then died.

Alerted by his agonized cries of death, Raul's shipmates stumbled from their bunks, groping about in the darkness for some means of defense against their unseen enemy. Steel flashed, meeting bone. A severed hand tumbled into the lap of a sailor still sitting in his bunk. Something warm and wet splattered against the startled sailor's face.

Howls of pain came shrieking from the corner as the mutilated man clamped his right hand over the stub of his left wrist. A fountain of red rained through his fingers. One of the black-clad killers dispatched the sailor with a blurring slash of his *katana*, the sword's razor-sharp blade cleanly lopping off the sailor's head, which rolled from its owner's shoulders and bounced across the floor.

The remaining sailors met their respective ends in much the same manner. Weaving their *katana* before them, the black-clad killers attacked, launching themselves at their victims in a frenzy of destruction.

Limbs fell, hearts were punctured. Bellies were sliced open like so many overripe melons. And then it was over. In less than a minute, fully a third of the ship's crew had been slaughtered.

Another five minutes reduced the *Bruja del Mar* to virtual ghost-ship status. Only Ferris and Mitchell were left alive. No one else, including the five remaining Americans who were butchered in their sleep, or Emilio Huerta, captain of the ship, had been spared.

At the bow of the *Bruja del Mar*, Lieutenant Daniel Mitchell sighed with relief.

"How 'bout that, Ferris? I can't hear any more hollering. Didn't even hear a single gunshot, come to think of it. Damn, but it looks like we pulled it off!"

"We sure did," Ferris agreed, then drove the blade of his knife as deep as he could into Mitchell's stomach.

Mitchell grunted and doubled over, clamping his hands over the hole in his gut when Ferris yanked the knife free.

"Wh...wh...why, Ferris?" Mitchell gasped, clenching his teeth. "We were supposed to be in this together. Why?"

"Just doubling my share of the profits," Ferris explained honestly, grinning as he tore the amulet bearing the three-headed snake from his former partner's neck, then stiff-arming Mitchell over the bulwark and into the sea.

As Ferris sheathed his knife and turned around he discovered that the leader of the black-clad attack force was standing before him. The man bowed politely to Ferris.

"It is done," the man said. "The ship is ours."

"Excellent," Ferris observed, returning the bow. "You and your men are to be congratulated."

The Oriental warrior introduced himself. "I am Sadatoshi Matsuno."

"Lieutenant Robert Ferris," the ONI man offered.

"And your compatriot?" Matsuno glanced to the left and right.

"Shark food." Ferris presented Matsuno with the medallion Mitchell had worn. "Lieutenant Mitchell is dead."

Sadatoshi Matsuno received the amulet adorned with the three-headed snake. "Most regrettable. Please accept my condolences."

"Accepted," Ferris said. "I wouldn't have it any other way."

2

Hal Brognola was preparing to torch the end of his unlit cigar when the call he had been expecting came through. He knew without question the identity of the person contacting him. The telephone that was ringing served as a direct and ultrasecure link with the White House.

Brognola set aside the box of wooden matches, then lifted the receiver to his ear.

"Yes, Mr. President?" the nation's top Fed answered.

"Good evening, Hal." The commander in chief's voice sounded particularly weary that night. "Putting in some overtime, I see."

"You know how I feel, sir. It's best to have a clean slate come Monday morning."

The President paused. "Not this time, I'm afraid. Something's come up."

"The incident concerning the disappearance of the *Bruja del Mar*, sir?"

Brognola thought he could hear the President smiling.

"You're always well on top of things, Hal, but yes. The *Bruja del Mar* is more than twelve hours overdue for its scheduled docking in Manila. A full-scale air-and-sea search has been launched out of Clark and Subic Bay, but so far they've come up empty. As far as we've been able to ascertain, the *Bruja del Mar* has simply vanished off the face of the earth."

Brognola glanced down at a computer printout he had been looking at minutes earlier. "I've examined the weather reports for the area over the past twenty-four hours. They show some pretty nasty activity. Any chance the ship went down in a storm?"

"That possibility is being investigated, of course, but we're giving it a low probability rating. The Colombians on board were all experienced sailors. The ship's captain was equally well-suited for his duties. The weather the *Bruja del Mar* would have encountered was nothing her crew couldn't handle."

"What about the others, sir?" Brognola asked, wishing now he had lit his cigar. "My reports show that the Colombian government had tendered a request for additional security from us. I'm assuming we complied."

"Through the ONI division in Guam," the President confirmed. "We lent the Colombians two senior officers, plus a contingent of a dozen men under their command. Which is why I'm contacting you. If something *has* happened to the Bruja del Mar while she was under our protection, the repercussions could be devastating."

"Such as derailing the treaty proposed by Senator Brandywine?" guessed Brognola.

"Precisely. The treaty establishes new guidelines for the Colombian government's increased crackdown on the manufacture and trafficking of illegal drugs in that country. We can't afford to have anything jeopardize it. The treaty's passage will sharply curtail the exportation and distribution of drugs in this country. It *must* go through."

"I understand, Mr. President," Brognola said, then added, "I would imagine Colombia's also anxious to learn what's happened to the *Bruja del Mar*'s cargo." He studied a copy of the ship's manifest. "She had enough gold and jewels on board to finance a small army."

"That's not how I like to picture it," admitted the President, "but of course, you're right. In the wrong hands the *Bruja del Mar*'s treasure could do great harm. In any event, I want you to put your people on this at once."

"I've already placed three of the five on standby alert. I'll notify them we definitely have a green light."

"Excellent." The President sounded relieved. "And the other two members of the team?"

"I'll have them on the horn within the hour," the Fed promised. "Will that be all, sir?"

"That should do it for now. It appears your Stony Man superstars may get the opportunity to bail us out of hot water again, Hal. Let them know they have my full support to do whatever it takes to put this matter to rest. Goodbye, Hal."

"Goodbye, Mr. President."

Brognola waited for the line to go dead, then hung up. He reached for his matches and lit his cigar, reflecting momentarily on the importance of the President's final statement.

Not too long ago, the entire Stony Man operation had been in danger of being scrapped. Now, however, those dark days were a million miles away.

The Stony Man program had originally been created to utilize the unique talents of one man, the fearless champion of justice known to the world as the Executioner. Mack Bolan was the Executioner. He alone had dared to square off against the evil and corruption that was the Mafia. He alone had dared combat an enemy whose numbers seemed endless, to wage a one-man war most would have deemed impossible to win.

Yet Bolan had triumphed. Through the gut-wrenching hell of thirty-eight campaigns he fought, bringing death and destruction to the Mafia's doorstep, unflinchingly meeting the powerful dons on their own turf, but with a new set of rules.

And when at last the smoke of that final battle had cleared, Mack Bolan emerged victorious. The backbone of the Mafia was broken. The Executioner had won his war.

But as old enemies retreated to lick their wounds and count their dead, a newer, even deadlier threat to humanity was rearing its murderous head. International terrorism was the latest cancer to infect the world, and the President of the United States called upon Bolan's battle-honed skills to deal with the modern-day savages in a language they could understand.

Bolan accepted the President's challenge and the supersecret Stony Man operation was born. Mack Bolan was listed as officially killed in action and, from the ashes of his past, was resurrected as Colonel John Phoenix.

Stony Man Farm served as headquarters for Colonel Phoenix and his allies, the elite commando units of Phoenix Force and Able Team. While Able Team consisted of three veterans from Bolan's decisive campaign against the Mafia, the warriors of Phoenix Force had been selected from the best the free world had to offer.

Five men were chosen. Special men. Handpicked by Bolan himself to serve as a new foreign legion. Five who fought with the fury of five hundred. Five brave soldiers who could accomplish what the might of governments and countries could not.

Hal Brognola was tapped as the liaison between the President and all Stony Man operations. His appointment was a natural for the nation's foremost federal agent. Brognola had cultivated a delicate alliance with Mack Bolan since the onset of the Executioner's war with the Mafia, and he welcomed the opportunity to work with his trusted friend in an operation sanctioned by the highest authority in the United States.

Stony Man was an instant success, an effective response to the arrogance of terrorism wherever it appeared. Yet, while its string of victories grew, the ultimate price paid for such a remarkable record was measured in blood.

Mack Bolan's woman, April Rose, and Stony Man's weapons expert, Andrzej Konzaki, perished in an attack on the headquarters. Aaron Kurtzman, computer expert for the organization, also fell, barely escaping with his life. The valiant Kurtzman would spend the rest of his days confined to a wheelchair.

Sadly, the sweet taste of success was further soured by an unfortunate series of events that caused Mack Bolan to sever all ties with Stony Man and the United States. "Colonel Phoenix" was branded a renegade, and every major law enforcement and intelligence network on both sides of the iron curtain had declared open season on him.

The fate of Stony Man's future hung in the balance after Bolan's sudden departure. Not even the President was convinced the bold experiment in antiterrorism should continue. But Hal Brognola stuck to his guns, his faith in the men of Phoenix Force and Able Team undeterred, his steadfast conviction that Stony Man had to survive at all costs an unwavering rock of determination.

Stony Man *had* endured, and ever since, the men under Brognola's command had rewarded their leader's trust in them by bravely confronting the enemies of freedom and decency with a fierce dedication second to none.

Now, Brognola reflected, the men of Phoenix Force were once again being called upon to risk their lives. The chief Fed knew his crack unit of antiterrorist commandos would not let him down.

THE TWO MEN EXITED the Cinema Six complex at the Long Beach Marina Mall, making their way to the parking lot where they had left their rented Thunderbird. It was Saturday night in Southern California. The moon was a wedge of yellow in the clear evening sky. An offshore breeze had pushed most of the day's smog away from the city.

"Great film," one of the men commented, his East London accent somehow well at home with the rumpled gray sweat shirt and faded blue Levi's he wore. "It always drives me potty how her Majesty's finest secret agent can save the universe from everything shy of an invasion from Mars and still wear a suit and tie for most of the movie."

The Londoner's companion, a tall lanky black man with black hair trimmed short, was quick to defend the character in the film.

"What're you talking about, David?" the black man wanted to know. "That suit-and-tie routine is part of old 007's mystique. The dude gets away with it 'cause he only has to save the world once every two years. If he had to tussle with trouble on a regular basis like a couple of guys I could name, you can bet your British boots he'd change tailors."

"You're right there, mate," David McCarter agreed, lighting a Player's cigarette that he'd pulled from the pack in his pocket. "And he wouldn't smile so much, either. You think his teeth are capped, Calvin?"

Calvin James grinned at McCarter. "Bonded in gold."

David McCarter and Calvin James represented two-fifths of the dynamic Phoenix Force team. They had journeyed to the West Coast for a breather and well-earned R&R after their latest mission in India had been completed. Taking in the motion-picture premiere of the newest entry in a spy series that had been running since 1962 was McCarter's idea. Both men had found the comic-book atmosphere of the movie an entertaining departure from the high level of tension they usually lived under.

David McCarter had spent most of his thirty-five years living the kind of life Hollywood screenwriters of adventure films could only dream about. Often short-tempered and high-strung when his energies were not being channeled on the battlefield, McCarter was the flesh-and-blood embodiment of the proud British lion.

Raised in London's colorful but tough East End, the hard-nosed Cockney had taken his knocks since day one. Considered handsome by most, the fox-faced Englishman was a superbly trained antiterrorist of the highest caliber.

A veteran of Great Britain's Strategic Air Service, McCarter was a former national champion of the British pistol marksmanship team, an expert in practically every form of combat and an excellent pilot.

Prior to his recruitment to Phoenix Force, McCarter had seen action in Southeast Asia, worked undercover for two years against Communist subversives in the British colony of Hong Kong, was stationed in Oman during the Omani Ohofar War and had participated in the SAS raid on the Iranian embassy in 1980.

"*Bonded* in gold?" McCarter repeated. "Is that what passes for humor in Chicago?"

Calvin James shrugged. "*Anything* passes for humor in Chicago."

"Bloody hell!"

Calvin James was the newest addition to Stony Man's Phoenix Force superpros having signed on for the duration shortly before Keio Ohara, one of the team's original five members, was slain battling the threat of the infamous Black Alchemists.

James was a product of Chicago's rough South Side, born in a gritty poverty-stricken neighborhood where children grew up fighting if they wanted to grow up at all.

Calvin James enlisted in the U.S. Navy at age seventeen where he trained as a hospital corpsman. The skills he exhibited there caught the attention of the SEALs, and eventually lead to his spending two years attached to a special operations group in Vietnam. Wounded during his final SOG mission, James was decorated for his courage and returned to the United States with an honorable discharge.

The years following his discharge saw James lose most of the members of his immediate family to one tragedy after another. His father died from a heart attack and his mother at the hands of muggers. A younger brother was listed as MIA in Vietnam. His sister died from a heroin overdose while still a junior-high-school student. His only surviving sibling was a doctor who lived with his wife and two children in Indianapolis.

James has been studying medicine and chemistry at UCLA in Los Angeles under the G.I. Bill, but after the deaths of his mother and sister, he switched to police science. Later he joined the San Francisco Police Department where his outstanding background made him an ideal candidate for the SWAT team. His superlative record brought him to the attention of Hal Brognola and Phoenix Force. The rest is history.

Calvin James may have been the newest addition to Stony Man's supersquad, but he fought alongside the rest of the Force as though he had been with them since the cradle.

McCarter and James reached the rented Thunderbird, James sliding behind the wheel, McCarter riding shotgun. They immediately heard an almost imperceptible beeping noise coming from the glove compartment.

"Looks like the vacation's over, mate," McCarter surmised, flipping open the glove box. Nestled neatly inside were two of the computerized marvels developed by Aaron "The Bear" Kurtzman.

The "beeping" object was a small rectangular piece of red plastic that could have been mistaken for a deck of cards. In fact, the simplistic-looking device was a highly sophisticated SFPL—a satellite fixed-point locater enabling Stony Man HQ to determine its whereabouts to within a quarter-mile-square area, virtually anywhere on the face of the earth.

McCarter deactivated the SFPL's alarm by pressing a small button at the back of the device, then reached inside the glove compartment and removed its computerized companion: a cellular communications receivertransmitter half the size of a paperback book. McCarter punched out a code on the receiver's twelve-digit keypad so that Stony Man would know to begin transmission, plugged in the earpiece and waited several seconds before the linkup between both parties was made.

"Good evening." Hal Brognola's voice came through the earpiece with uncanny clarity. "Long Beach is nice this time of year."

"Ah, Uncle Samuel," McCarter answered, opting to keep mum on Brognola's real identity, "so nice to hear from you." Although transmissions in and out of Stony Man were routed through a special communications satellite equipped with a scrambler, the former SAS man saw no need to violate security unless absolutely necessary. "How's the family doing these days?"

"That's why I called," Brognola replied. "I was thinking of arranging a reunion. Your cousins are anxious to see you again. So am I."

"That shouldn't be a problem. I'm sure we could catch a flight home no trouble at all."

"No, no, don't do that," Brognola insisted. "It's been so long since we've seen California, I'd much prefer bringing the family with me."

McCarter nodded. "Sounds good to us, uncle. Anytime."

"We'll be on the next plane to LAX. Like I said, this reunion's important to all of us. You and your brother haven't moved since the last time I talked to you?"

"Not us, uncle. You and the boys fly out as soon as you can. We'll keep the porch light on."

"Sounds good," the Fed said, then added, "Try and keep your noses clean until we arrive."

The transmission from Stony Man Farm ended and McCarter returned the handset to its place in the glove compartment.

"What did 'Uncle Samuel' want?" James asked.

"A reunion. He's flying out with Katz and the rest on the first available flight to L.A."

"Do tell," Calvin said, noticing a young couple walking arm in arm through the parking lot two rows over. "Any hints as to *why* the emergency get-together?"

"Hal says he misses us."

"So tell him to phone more often."

"He also says to keep our noses clean until he arrives."

Calvin's voice turned icy. "Hal's shit outta luck on that account, David. My gut tells me we've just inherited a big bad problem."

"Where?" McCarter snapped.

James pointed. "Next to that van two rows up. I was watching a guy and his girl walking across the parking lot. They crossed between the van and the car next to it, then *nada*. That's the last I saw of them. Maybe...?"

"Damn right we should!" McCarter exclaimed, jumping from the Thunderbird and getting halfway to where the van was parked before James caught up with him.

"Hey, take it easy. I might be wrong. For all I know they could've slipped into the back of the van to test the rear shocks."

McCarter shook his head. "You're not wrong, Cal. You read the signs right. Those kids are in some kind of trouble. What're you carrying?"

James patted the outside of his sports coat near the right shoulder. "Everything I need."

McCarter responded by holding up a pair of clenched fists. "Me, too."

They were less than fifteen yards from the van when they heard it—the muffled scream of a female, quickly followed by the harsh sound of an open palm slapping against bare flesh.

Galvanized into action by the stifled scream, the two Phoenix Force soldiers raced to the rescue, rounding the bumper at the rear of the van to hear the girl scream again. Four men, each appearing to be in their late teens to early twenties, stood outside the van while one or more of their pals went to work on the helpless girl inside. Her

boyfriend was unconscious and sprawled under the
wheels of a Toyota truck nearby.

One of the rapists-in-waiting saw the Phoenix Force
duo appear, but had no chance to warn his buddies as
McCarter and James attacked, slamming into the punks
blocking their way like two locomotives crashing through
a depot made of toothpicks. Shouting and swearing in
surprise and anger, the four hoods tumbled to the
ground.

One attacker started to his feet, but Calvin stopped him
cold, putting him to sleep with a vicious kick to the side
of the head that broke the tough's jaw and sent bloody
Chiclets of broken teeth spraying from his mouth. The
slob fell to the cement like a wet sack of dirt.

McCarter reached into the van and grabbed for the
half-naked slimeball trying to rape the girl. The startled
attacker had been busy working his victim's thighs apart
when the Briton's steely grip put the creep's passion on
hold.

McCarter's right hand dug into the thug's sensitive
shoulder muscles, while his left hand captured a handful
of the hood's stringy hair. The Englishman yanked in reverse and the man went flying, sailing from the interior
of the van to smash against the side of the Toyota truck
outside.

The stunned pile of garbage struggled to free himself
from McCarter's grasp as the Briton suddenly pivoted,
spinning the guy in a rapid semicircle that ended when the
hoodlum's face collided with the passenger window of
the Japanese 4x4. The window withstood the punishment as the hood's nose mashed to the consistency of
strawberry jelly and left a smearing streak that painted
the side of the truck all the way to the pavement.

"David!"

McCarter heeded Calvin's warning as a brass-knuckled fist zoomed at him from behind. He ducked, dropping to his left as the knuckle-duster continued overhead, striking the 4x4's window. This time the glass shattered, spiderwebbing into a hole large enough to swallow the attacker's fist to several inches past the wrist.

McCarter struck, hammering an elbow into his assailant's back, propelling the body forward, forcing the man's head into the window and through the already shattered glass. The body twitched like a fish hanging from a hook and went still.

While McCarter was dealing with his share of the trash from the van, the two remaining hoods climbed to their feet and brandished a couple of switchblades in Calvin's direction.

"Step away from the van, asshole," one of the knife-wielding toughs snarled, "or we're gonna carve your black hide up one side and down the other."

"Try it, shit face," James said with a laugh, whipping out the G-96 Boot 'n' Belt knife he carried in a sheath attached to the Jackass Leather rig under his right arm. James was well versed in the use of all kinds of knives, a talent he acquired during his Wonder Bread years in Chicago "You fuckers want some action tonight. Come with me."

The fool who threatened Calvin was stupid enough to go for it, yelling some half-assed cry he had probably picked up from television as he charged. Calvin avoided the sloppy assault and countered with the deadly G-96. The double-edged blade sank into his opponent's unprotected side, cracking through a rib and puncturing the loser's left lung.

Calvin withdrew the G-96 as the wheezing loudmouth dropped his switchblade and began squealing like a stuck pig. James was tempted to tickle the guy again with the business end of the sturdy Boot 'n' Belt, but reversed the knife at the last second so the punk could check out thanks to a blow on the skull from the G-96's steel butt.

James stood away as the body flopped to the ground in a lifeless heap, then flashed a smile to the final hood with the switchblade.

"You're next, Junior." Calvin held up the G-96. "Come take your medicine."

At which point Junior threw down his switchblade and ran...straight into one of the hardest punches David McCarter had ever enjoyed throwing. McCarter's target crumpled to the pavement without a sound.

"Guess that cuts it," James stated, sheathing the G-96. Already they could hear the screams of police sirens approaching in a rush. "Great. Somebody called the cops. Publicity's the last thing we want. Brognola's gonna be pissed for sure."

"What about?" McCarter asked. "We *kept* our noses clean."

"Yeah," Calvin agreed. "And that's about all."

3

After observing that certain individuals, and one former SAS commando in particular, had done one hell of a lousy job keeping their noses clean as ordered, Brognola went on to congratulate McCarter and James for their performance in the parking lot. Thanks to their combined efforts, the couple who had been attacked were recovering from their ordeal at Long Beach General Hospital.

Also thanks to the timely intervention, six would be rapists were now in police custody. All were suffering from a multitude of external and internal injuries. Two of the hoodlums were on the critical list.

In Brognola's estimation, the punks responsible for the assault were lucky. Considering the damage McCarter and James *could* have inflicted on the six, it was a wonder to the Fed they were alive at all.

Brognola and the complete Phoenix Force team were assembled in the Holiday Inn suite where McCarter and James had been staying. Once a sweep was performed to make certain the room was free of any electronic bugs, Brognola got down to business, informing the Force of all he knew concerning the disappearance of the Colombian ship *Bruja del Mar*.

"*Bruja del Mar*," Rafael Encizo commented for the benefit of the two members of the unit who did not speak Spanish, "translates to 'Witch of the Sea.'"

Encizo, a stocky, muscular Cuban with good looks and a ready smile, was a veteran of the Bay of Pigs invasion. Taken prisoner by the Communists, he was sentenced to El Principe, Cuba's infamous prison for political enemies of the Castro regime.

Starved and beaten, Encizo was subjected to the torturous skills of Russian "technicians" who attempted to reeducate and recondition his beliefs to their way of thinking. Rafael played along with his captors until his chance for escape came. He broke a guard's neck and broke out of the prison.

Returning to the United States, Encizo became a naturalized citizen, eventually finding employment as an insurance investigator specializing in maritime claims. Prior to that, his various occupations included stints as a treasure hunter, scuba instructor and professional bodyguard.

Fanatically loyal to his friends and totally ruthless to his enemies, Rafael Encizo had served as a fearless member of the Phoenix Force team since its inception.

"With that kind of cargo," Gary Manning noted, "she may as well have been named 'Bank of the Sea.'"

Gary Manning, the Force's best rifleman, had served as a lieutenant in the Canadian army where he specialized in explosives and quickly earned a reputation as one of the finest demolition experts in the world. His military duty included a tour in Vietnam where his role in that conflict was officially listed as "observer."

Manning's true reason for being in Nam involved work with the 5th Special Forces and the clandestine Special Observations Group where his highly regarded talents as a demo man were put to use destroying numerous NVA bases. Manning was one of a handful of Canadians to receive the Silver Star for valor from the United States.

Following Vietnam, the barrel-chested workaholic signed up with the RCMP, which led in time to a position in their antiterrorist division. As his reputation for tackling every task he faced with bulldog determination grew, Manning found himself assigned to Europe where he worked in conjunction with the elite GSG-9 antiterrorists of West Germany.

When the Royal Canadian Mounted Police pulled out of the espionage game, the newly formed Canadian Security Intelligence Service offered Manning a desk job. He refused, choosing instead to enter the private sector, marry and raise a family. The marriage ended in divorce, but Manning's business career excelled without missing a beat. He was employed as a security consultant and junior executive of North America International when Stony Man and Phoenix Force entered his life.

Colonel Yakov Katzenelenbogen, senior member and unit commander of the team, leaned forward in his chair. "This 'Sea Witch' is precisely the kind of bank our assorted enemies would love to crack. The exorbitant richness of her cargo could help finance a wealth of horrors."

Katzenelenbogen resembled anything but one of the world's foremost antiterrorists. With his iron-gray hair, paunchy midsection and gentle blue eyes, the middle-aged Israeli looked more like a professor. Only the fact that his right arm had been amputated at the elbow came close to betraying Yakov's genuine line of work.

Actively involved with warfare, espionage and antiterrorism since he was a teenager, Katzenelenbogen served in Europe with the Resistance fighters against the

Nazis. Beyond the Second World War, he gained further experience in the Haganah against the British when Israel was still fighting for independence and continued with the Mossad afterward.

Katz had lost his right arm in the Six Day War; the same bloody conflict that had claimed the life of his son.

"Are we absolutely sure the *Bruja del Mar* didn't simply sink in a storm?" Calvin asked.

"We are now," admitted Brognola, his smoking cigar jammed to the side of his mouth like a leafy torpedo. "Additional information that's become available since the President first assessed me of the situation virtually eliminates that possibility."

"What kind of 'additional information' is that?" McCarter quizzed, as eager as any of the Force to get to the bottom of the Colombian ship's mysterious disappearance. "Don't tell me the *Bruja del Mar* has been seen in a port other than Manila?"

The Fed frowned. "No, not that easy. What has occurred is that several art objects known to have been part of the *Bruja del Mar*'s cargo have been offered for sale to one of Manila's top fences."

"Shit!" Manning swore. "That proves the ship was hit. If some of the treasure's starting to surface already, then you can be sure the *Bruja del Mar* ran into the wrong kind of trouble."

"And it gets worse," Brognola advised. "I explained how the Office of Naval Intelligence was enlisted by the Colombian government to provide additional security for the cruise. Prior to our departure to Los Angeles, I received an updated background check on all ONI personnel assigned to the *Bruja del Mar*. It contained a startling piece of news. The report showed that both senior officers of the ONI security detail, a Lieutenant Ferris and a

Lieutenant Mitchell, had recently accrued heavy gambling debts."

"Which would make them ideal candidates for a quick cash loan under the table," Encizo concluded. "And once they accepted the bail-out money, somebody other than ONI could be calling their tune."

Brognola sighed. "Apparently, you're one hundred percent correct. Gambling debts of both officers *were* paid in full by an unspecified third party."

"That cuts it then," McCarter said, jumping into the conversation. "The bastards were bought off. They sold out for money. Second oldest story in the world."

"It looks that way," Brognola said. "At any rate, if you can manage to track down Ferris and Mitchell, then we'll have a handle on what happened to the *Bruja del Mar*."

Manning offered, "It sounds like we're talking about piracy on the high seas, in which case it's a fair bet that if these two ONI lieutenants *are* involved, then they had to have plenty of help."

"Considering the priceless pre-Columbian art objects and jewels on board the ship, I'm surprised something like this hasn't happened sooner." Katz wrapped the fingers of his left hand around the base of the prosthetic three-pronged hook he usually favored. "Gary's right, though. Pulling off a stunt this size, and doing so without leaving much of a trail, would require the concentrated efforts of a large, well-trained strike force. Any guesses?"

"Modern-day pirates do ply their trade within the waters surrounding the Philippines," Brognola informed the group. "And when they're not stealing from the locals, they make ends meet by running guns from

Borneo to the Communists opposing the Philippine government.''

"I know about the pirates," McCarter said. "A pack of cowards. But I always thought they pretty much stuck to themselves. Taking on a haul like the *Bruja del Mar* seems out of their league."

"Not only that," Brognola added, "but out of their territory, too. The pirates we know about usually stick to the waters between Borneo and Mindanao, while the *Bruja del Mar*'s last known location was approximately sixty to eighty miles off the Philippine coast, over what's known as the Philippine Trench."

Calvin whistled. "That's a piss-poor spot to run into trouble. The Trench is more than six and a half miles deep."

"A perfect location to stage an attack," Katz said. "Once the *Bruja del Mar* was relieved of her treasure, as is obviously the case, and if those responsible for the assault wanted to sink the ship, they couldn't choose a better place."

"And against the odds that every man on board suddenly went the Jolly Roger route—" Manning brought the discussion full circle "—there's every reason to suspect that most, if not all, of the ship's Colombian crew is past caring about whether or not the treasure's been stolen."

"Right, Gary," Brognola cut in. "And that's why I've booked seats for all of you on the next PAL flight out of Manila. None of your luggage will be subject to a search here in Los Angeles, so pack heavy. Also, don't worry about having to cope with a custom's inspection once you reach the Philippines. There won't be any inspection. Since some of the art taken from the *Bruja del Mar* has turned up for sale in Manila, it's the obvious place to begin your investigation.''

McCarter made a sour face. "Investigation? It doesn't take the five of us to play detective. What are we supposed to do when we find what we're looking for? Sit back and write a book about it? That doesn't sound too exciting.''

"I'm not suggesting a soft probe," Brognola told them. "Your orders are to do whatever it takes to recover the *Bruja del Mar*'s treasure. If you have to kick over some stones to find the snakes at the bottom of all this, that's your decision. It's totally up to you. And that comes straight from the man in the White House.

"The U.S. is finalizing negotiations with the Colombian government for an enhanced crackdown program aimed at cutting off the production of illicit drugs at their point of manufacture in Colombia. If the stuff isn't produced, it can't be exported north into the States. The President would hate to see anything spoil the negotiations. I assured him that you would feel the same.''

McCarter jumped to his feet, enthusiastically rubbing his hands together. "Now *that*'s more like it!''

"I hate when you get that sound in your voice," Manning complained.

"Don't start feeling like the Lone Ranger," Encizo advised the Englishman.

"Leave off," McCarter protested. "I'm just excited, that's all. A mate of mine from when I worked in Hong Kong retired to Manila. This will give me a chance to see him again. I'll call him when we arrive. Maybe he can help us out.''

"If he's anything like you," Manning grumbled, "I'm not so sure.''

4

It was a time for celebration.

The assault upon the Colombian ship had been performed with flawless precision. The treasure was theirs, and soon the whims of the avaricious West would magnify that cache to richness overflowing. The wisdom of their union would not be denied. The glory and strength that was TRIO could not be contained.

Delicate chimes sounded three times and the black-clad warriors who had taken the Colombian ship's treasure for their own filed noiselessly into the vast chamber of rough-hewn stone. Torches hanging from the ceiling burned brightly, filling the chamber with fiery hues, painting the walls of the refurbished, hundred-year-old Spanish fortress with a parade of dancing shadows.

The chimes rang again and the black-clad figures ceased to move, standing as they were in equal rows of twelve men each. With their heads bowed in humble respect, they presented themselves before a great wooden platform that had been carved from the trunk of a single tree.

Three magnificent chairs, ornate thrones of red Philippine mahogany, were stationed on the platform. Folds of intricately woven embroidered silk draped each chair, and directly behind them a variety of Oriental tapestries were displayed.

The fabric murals depicted scenes that had long in-spired the chroniclers of legend and lore. Among the scenes featured was the Great Wall of China, the beau-tiful Daibutsu-den, or "Great Buddha Hall," in the heart of the city of Nara and finally the spectacle of ferocious Mongol horsemen led by Genghis Khan.

The musical chimes sounded for yet a third time and the luxurious curtain formed by the tapestries was drawn apart, allowing TRIO's illustrious leaders to appear upon the platform. In silence they crossed to their respective thrones and sat, patiently observing the ritual of the vic-tory ceremony.

TRIO represented the insidious merger of three sepa-rate criminal networks: the Black Serpent Tong of China, the Snake Clan of the Japanese *yakuza*, and the dreaded New Horde of Mongolia. By setting aside their preju-dices and mistrust, the rivals of centuries had overcome their differences to merge as one, making TRIO the most powerful organization of its kind in the Orient.

Seated in the center chair upon the wooden platform was Wang tse Tu, the *ling shyou* or leader of the Yi-chyun Hai Shoo the Black Serpent Tong. An obese man of enormous proportions, Wang was attired in a yellow dragon robe with a long burgundy jacket. The decora-tive court collar he wore towered above his head, upon which sat a cap adorned with a peacock-feather tassle.

His eyes were like knife slits set in his smooth round face. His stringy gray beard and mandarin mustache only added to his Chinese warlord image, as did the square-shaped *pu fang* hanging around his neck. A three-headed snake against a gold background dominated the amulet.

Wang tse Tu did nothing by half measures.

The Black Serpent Tong traced its heritage back to 1646 when numerous secret tong societies in China bat-

tled to overthrow the tyranny of the Manchu Dynasty.
Infighting and the lack of manpower ultimately prevented the tongs from ousting the Manchus as planned,
but not before their political aspirations had been abandoned for a life of crime.

White slavery, murder for hire and the burgeoning op-
ium trade all fell under the tong's sphere of influence.
Nor were the profits to be gained from prostitution and
gambling overlooked. If the vice dealt with fear, greed or
lust for hire, the secret societies of the Chinese tong were
sure to be involved.

When Chinese settlers migrated to the New World and
Western Europe, the evil of the tong went with them, infesting new corners of the globe. With the expansion, the
Black Serpent Society became one of the few truly international tong networks, its power more pronounced than
any other tong's, save for the Brothers of Heaven and
Earth—better known as the Triad.

The Black Serpent's first base in the United States was
San Francisco's Chinatown district in the early 1850s.
Other tongs had the same idea and in the years that followed, full-scale tong wars transformed San Francisco's
streets into rivers of blood. The wars ended in 1860 only
after a truce was negotiated and the tong's Five Companies were formed, predating by nearly a century the so-
called Five Families of the Mafia.

Named after the five provinces of China, the Companies constituted the elite ruling class of tong activities in
San Francisco. Rival sects were abolished or absorbed as
the strength of the Black Serpent society, one of the Five
Companies, prospered and grew.

In the ensuing years, tong operations continued to
spread throughout the United States, with society busi-

ness rarely carried out beyond the boundaries of Chinese districts.

Wang tse Tu settled his great bulk into his seat and was pleased. The victories of his tong's magnificent past were but a prelude for the bountiful glories still to come.

Sitting to the right of Wang was Shimo Goro, *obyan* of the Hebi Uji—the Snake Clan. The black kimono and obi of gold that the middle-aged Japanese wore did not disguise his powerful shoulders and thick expansive chest, muscles he had developed through many years of *kenjutsu* sword-fighting and other martial arts. A pale greencolored fan held by the obi and *hakama* collots rounded out Shimo Goro's ornate wardrobe.

A *katana* rested against the armrest of Shimo's throne, ever within reach. This particular *katana* had been fashioned by Hashigo Haifu, a master Japanese swordmaker of the thirteenth century, and had once belonged to the great samurai warrior Shimo Karada, who became a renegade *ronin* and later a *yakuza*.

Traditionally, possession of the famous *katana* was a symbol and legacy of leadership of *yakuza* for the proud Shimo family. Shimo Goro had inherited his position as the Snake Clan's *obyan*, and he accepted his station in life as a sacred trust and an honored duty.

As did Wang tse Tu, Shimo Goro also wore the medallion of the triple-headed serpent around his neck.

The history of the Snake Clan began in feudal Japan when the *yakuza* were then known as "thieves with honor." Products of the lower classes, the *yakuza* were schooled in martial arts and swordsmanship by wandering *ronin*, renegade mercenary samurai.

During this period the *yakuza* enjoyed a reputation as Robin Hood-style champions of the poor, but in time their role as defenders of the oppressed gave way to less worthy endeavors. The *yakuza* clans surrendered to greed and became criminal organizations. Gunrunning, gambling and the rewards to be gained by controlling prostitution were all part of the *yakuza*'s stock and trade and, while most *obyan* refused to include the profits from the sale of narcotics in their business, some *yakuza* clans did sidestep the issue of honor among thieves by entering into the narcotics trade.

Following the Second World War, some of the more ambitious *obyan* extended their operations to the United States. But with competition from the Mafia and already established tongs, plus the growing opposition from black gangster groups and Spanish syndicates, the *yakuza* appeared helpless to pose any threat to the various organized crime forces in America.

But the criminal *yakuza* clans were patient and with the age of industrial expansion in Japan, many Tokyo-based, *yakuza*-owned businesses found themselves eagerly sought after as prospective partners by American corporations. By recruiting the aid of Japanese Americans to operate on par within a Western environment, the Snake Clan cultivated the financial support and business connections necessary to become a power inside the United States.

At the opposite end of the platform sat the Mongol, Tosha Khan. Not to be outdone by his contemporaries, Tosha Khan's wardrobe was easily as resplendent as theirs. With chain-mail bracelets attached to each wrist and forearm, a brass helmet decorated with horns strapped to his head, and a deep purple robe flocked with gold, the Mongolian leader of the New Horde, with his cunning face and drooping black mustache streaked with silver, looked every bit as fierce as his ancestors.

The metal breastplate on his chest was highlighted by the three-headed snake amulet that hung from his neck.

Born in the Mongolian capital of Ulan Bator and given the name Altajin Illyvich Dzadgad, Tosha Khan was descended of the Tartars and, as was believed by his family, could trace his lineage to a distant relative who had been a favored concubine of Genghis Khan.

This revelation was more than Altajin could have hoped for. Genghis Khan, the Mongol conqueror, had united the savage Mongol tribes and led his Golden Horde to claim an empire larger than any Alexander or the Caesars had ever possessed.

For two hundred years the Mongolian empire held sway over Russia, China and most of Eastern Europe. And while the passing of time had eroded the might of that most powerful empire, the exploits of Genghis Khan would forever be remembered.

Obsessed by his legendary heritage, young Altajin grew to hate the Communists who ruled the People's Republic of Mongolia as a mere extension of the Soviet Union. To his way of thinking, the Soviets had denied his legacy as an emperor by birthright.

So Altajin Illyvich Dzadgad ceased to exist and was reborn as Tosha Khan, a man dedicated to creating an empire to rule of his own design—an empire of crime. His was an organization of thieves and assassins, dope dealers, professional slavers and counterfeiters, and he proclaimed his network of evil the New Horde.

For forty years Tosha Khan journeyed throughout the world recruiting followers from all stratas of society. Most of the New Horde were Orientals or Eurasians of Mongolian descent. With branches in Asia, parts of Eastern Europe, Turkey, and even the Soviet Union, the ranks of Tosha Khan's shadow empire grew heavy with success.

Yet for all his efforts to establish the New Horde on an international basis, and despite the smaller operations in France, Spain and Italy, Tosha Khan realized that because it lacked the wealth, influence and well-placed connections that had taken the tong and *yakuza* centuries to develop, the New Horde would never become the empire of his dreams unless desperate steps were taken.

Thus, when the opportunity to merge with his former rivals presented itself, Tosha Khan accepted the terms of the merger and TRIO was created.

Wang tse Tu, Shimo Goro and Tosha Khan were TRIO's undisputed rulers. Through unification, their merciless partnership made TRIO a name to be feared by all.

FROM HIS VANTAGE POINT at the back of the rock-hewn hall, Lieutenant Robert Ferris, formerly with the Office of Naval Intelligence, watched TRIO's ritual celebration with interest. As a Westerner, Ferris knew that his being permitted to view the ceremony was no small honor and spoke highly of the regard TRIO felt for his help in capturing the *Bruja del Mar*'s treasure.

Ferris had heard of TRIO's leaders, but this was his first opportunity to see them in person. To those unfamiliar with the Oriental way of thinking—and Ferris did not fall into this category—the elaborate props and costumes used and worn by TRIO's overlords might have seemed ludicrous, behavior not befitting three criminal masterminds.

Lieutenant Ferris knew differently.

In the Orient all things held with reverence were deemed worthy of ritual conduct. To revere a thing and not respect its ceremonial value was a lie of the heart. Whether an activity was religious in nature, involved the military, the legal profession, business meetings, or something as simple in the private sector as properly preparing and serving a cup of tea, the importance of ritual and ceremony was an ever-present constant.

Ferris was impressed with the efficiency TRIO exhibited. There was no waste. Everyone fit neatly into the scheme of things, going about their respective tasks so the wheels of progress moved ever onward. He had witnessed the well-oiled machine that was TRIO in action the night the *Bruja del Mar* had been taken.

Once the threat of resistance from the Colombian crew and U.S. naval personnel had been eliminated, the factions Ferris had conspired with went to work. All of the bodies were deposited and packed into four separate compartments located on the middle deck of the ship. The compartments were closed and welded shut.

In the meantime, the *Bruja del Mar* was stripped of its precious cargo and its treasure was transferred to one of the three TRIO vessels nearby. Explosive charges were placed at strategic locations along the ship's hull, timed to explode five minutes after everyone had safely departed.

Ferris listened for the detonations, but the rising fury of the approaching storm drowned out any noise the explosive charges might have made. The only indication Ferris had that the timed blasts had gone off on schedule came when the *Bruja del Mar* suddenly listed to one side and began to sink.

It was the beginning of the end for the Colombian ship. Within minutes she was gone, lost beneath the angry waves of the Pacific. But her passing was not mourned. While it was true the *Bruja del Mar* and her crew had gone to a watery grave, the fabulous treasure Colombia's floating museum had carried was spared a similar fate.

And now TRIO was celebrating. Ferris savored the moment of delicious victory and observed as the ceremony continued.

For the fourth time that evening since TRIO's black-clad warriors had assembled in the chambered ruins of the Spanish fortress, the musical chimes were heard. The scent of jasmine incense was everywhere.

As the sound of the chimes began to fade, the soldiers of TRIO knelt before their emperors, waiting until the obese Wang slashed the air with the elongated fingernails of his riding hand, bidding them to rise.

"Stand tall, brave warriors of TRIO!" Wang announced in a booming voice that carried through the fortress chamber like thunder. "Stand tall! You have made your fathers proud."

Ferris had no difficulty comprehending what was said, for Wang spoke to his men in English; ironically, the only common language the Oriental crime lords shared.

"Upon this night your leaders salute you," Wang continued, and with that, TRIO's emperors rose slowly from their ornately decorated thrones and bowed in unison toward those who served them.

The response of the thirty-six champions dressed in black was immediate. No sooner had the TRIO leaders retaken their seats than their black-clad followers bowed once more in return...*much* lower than before.

"Good." Shimo Goro said after the men were standing upright again. "It is good." The Japanese *obyan*'s eyes glistened. "Let it be known upon this night that the treasure you have taken for TRIO shall seed the fields of our activities for many years to come."

Shimo paused, fingering the hilt of his beloved *katana*, his eyes singling out the foremost of the center row of men. "Sadatoshi Matsuno. Step forward."

The man obeyed instantly, moving a full two feet in front of the rest of the group.

"Your humble servant awaits your command, Shimo-*sama*." Matsuno bowed, having addressed the *yakuza* boss as "Lord Shimo."

"To you, Sadatoshi Matsuno, the responsibility of this most important mission was entrusted," Shimo Goro said. "As field commander for this operation, success or failure weighed upon your able shoulders. Not only did you seize control of the Colombian ship and secure her treasure as ours, but you succeeded in doing so without the loss of a single TRIO life. You are to be congratulated, Sadatoshi Matsuno, most humble servant of TRIO. You and all who enjoyed the benefit of your leadership in the field have earned the right to bask in the glorious satisfaction of a job well done."

"No!" Tosha Khan shouted loudly from his seat, his unexpected outcry prompting Shimo to wrap his fingers around the hilt of his *katana*, and the ponderous Wang to momentarily taste the traces of his morning meal. "Forgive my intervention, my brothers," the Mongol apologized, "but it would shame the honor of all true heroes of TRIO if I allowed this celebration to progress."

Shimo Goro's bushy eyebrows fairly bristled with rage. "What is this *shame* you speak of, Tosha Khan? I am sure I speak for Wang tse Tu when I confess that we haven't an inkling of what you are talking about!"

The Japanese *obyan* shook with such undisguised wrath that Ferris could easily picture the *yakuza* with the iron-gray hair leaping from his seat and striking down with his *katana* on the Mongol leader.

"You have expressed my sentiments precisely." Wang nodded politely to Shimo, then turned his attention to his Mongolian counterpart. "For reasons known only to you, Mr. Khan, you have elected to destroy the sanctity of this most special occasion. We who have journeyed so far and worked so diligently to reach this moment in time are most curious."

"And so I shall explain," said Tosha Khan. "So I shall explain."

He rose from his throne and stood facing his audience, the chain-mail bracelets bound to each wrist and forearm glimmering in the glow of the burning torches as he braced his hands against his sides.

"When I found it necessary to stop the festivities of this noble event," Tosha Khan began, "it was only a matter of coincidence that my good friend, Shimo Goro—" he spat the name from his mouth like a tough piece of meat he could not chew "—was engaged in his laudatory praise for his pupil Sadatoshi Matsuno. My interruption was *merely* a coincidence.

"I can assure Sadatoshi Matsuno that I intended no disrespect. He had performed admirably in the service of TRIO. It was Sadatoshi Matsuno who led the TRIO force on the assault of the Colombian treasure ship, and it was he who returned with the richness of that floating museum to fill TRIO's coffers."

Tosha Khan made a gesture in the air, looking to his left and right. "Why, we even have Sadatoshi Matsuno to thank for our current base of operations. Using only the smallest portion of the treasure from the *Bruja del Mar*, Sadatoshi Matsuno was able to buy our way into a stronghold that will safely harbor our forces *and* TRIO's newfound wealth until final arrangements for the redistribution and sale of that cache have been made.

"So, no...good friends of TRIO, I have not brought to a halt our ceremony tonight out of any disrespect for Sadatoshi Matsuno."

"So why *have* you seen fit to do this thing in the very middle of my speech?" Shimo Goro, annoyed and impatient, demanded, still trying to get to the bottom of Tosha Khan's strange behavior.

"The reason is simple," Tosha Khan said. "We all know that when the treasure from the Colombian ship was brought to this fortress hideaway, the gold and jewels were to be sealed within a makeshift vault inside this citadel of stone."

"To be stored there under guarded protection until such time when the gold and jewels are transferred," Wang added, as anxious as Shimo Goro to learn what Tosha Khan was driving at. "The orders for what was to be done with the cache have never been a secret."

"Agreed," said the Mongol warlord, "but what was *not* part of TRIO's plans for the treasure was that some of our *trusted* members would selfishly keep a share of that wealth for themselves."

"*Nani?*" Shimo Goro could no longer contain himself. "Someone within our ranks has taken the gold and the emeralds? Who would dare shame our brotherhood with such a crime?"

A murmur of surprise and displeasure swept the chamber as each of TRIO's soldiers exchanged suspicious glances with one another.

"Believe me, Lord Shimo," Tosha Khan continued, "that my shock and outrage matched your own, and while it is true that your disciple of the Hebi Uji, Sadatoshi Matsuno, is deserving of the praise he has received, it is *also* true that one of my men of the New Horde has done TRIO a great service by bringing the matter of the theft of our treasure to my attention.'' Khan paused, stroking his drooping black mustache. "I call for New Horde warrior and loyal TRIO champion Wulanji to step forward.''

A tall, thick-featured Mongol with wind-reddened skin and hands the size of bricks moved apart from the ranks of the black-clad fighters as commanded.

"You will tell Shimo Goro and Wang tse Tu what you told me,'' Tosha Khan ordered.

The man called Wulanji bowed. "After we had transported the treasure here to our fortress, I could not help but notice how two of the men who had participated in this grand adventure appeared to be up to something. I could not say for certain what made me suspect them, but nonetheless I decided to kccp an eye on them.

"Several hours later I followed as the pair left this stronghold for a walk in the woods surrounding this place. It was while watching from a distance that I was able to determine that the men had somehow managed to siphon off some of TRIO's property for their own selfish purposes. The miserable scoundrels had buried what they had stolen and were unable to resist the temptation of viewing their prizes once more. Thus, their reason for going into the forest.''

Tosha Khan was satisfied. "And the names of these two men?''

Wulanji did not hesitate. "On my honor and by the blood of my father, the perpetrators of this crime of crimes are Lang Hui and Song Zhiwu!''

Immediately, the accused broke from the column, attempting to make their escape...a futile gesture on their part given the ferocity upon which their TRIO brothers launched themselves at the fleeing pair. In a matter of seconds the two struggling Chinese were hauled to the front of the chamber and before the wrath of their emperors.

"By your own foolish bid at flight you have removed all doubt as to your guilt," Wang tse Tu pronounced as he lifted his enormous girth to a standing position. That the traitors to TRIO were Chinese was humiliation enough for the Black Serpent Society leader; that the knowledge of that miserable fact had come at the hands of one of Tosha Khan's barbarians was more than Wang could stomach.

Wang regarded the thieves with contempt. "The disgrace you have brought to this joyous celebration stuns my senses to the core." Wang's knife-slit eyes squinted even further. "I confess I can think of no punishment too severe for the likes of dogs such as you."

"Perhaps I could be of help?" Tosha Khan offered, almost prompting Lieutenant Ferris, observing what was happening from the rear of the chamber, to laugh out loud.

It was obvious to Ferris that the Mongolian's popularity with Shimo Goro and Wang tse Tu was rocketing to an all time low, yet the ONI renegade could not help admiring how Tosha Khan forged onward, totally aware of the tension he was causing.

"Please, Tosha Khan—" Wang turned a weary eye to the Mongol "—don't trouble yourself. Bringing this horrific matter to our attention is more than we can ask of you."

"Nonsense," Khan said. "I *insist*."

"Very well," Shimo Goro jumped in, coming to Wang's aid. There was nothing much of the evening's celebration to salvage, and the *yakuza obyan* was eager to be done with the whole revolting business. "Tell us,

Tosha Khan. What punishment would you mete out to these animals who have betrayed us?''

Tosha Khan spoke. "Simply this: I would banish both traitors from the ranks of TRIO forever."

The faces of the Chinese thieves held captive in front of the emperor's platform brightened. While forced retirement from TRIO *was* regrettable, it was *also* more desirable than enduring the punishment their crime warranted.

"Out of the question!" Wang announced as he digested Tosha Khan's proposal.

"And," Khan went on, "I would have these lowly criminals take that which they have stolen with them."

"Madness!" Shimo Goro growled, but Tosha Khan was not to be swayed from his decision.

"I assure you, Lord Shimo, that the punishment I have proposed most equitably fits the crime. I ask only that you and Wang tse Tu support me in this. I would not shame TRIO more by passing a sentence that was unworthy of our brotherhood. Well?"

Shimo Goro shifted his gaze from Tosha Khan to Wang. The overweight leader of the tong pursed his bowlike mouth in disgust, but did not protest Tosha Khan's proposal.

Shimo Goro sighed. "Very well, Tosha Khan. It shall be as you say."

"Excellent." The Mongol chieftain turned his attention to the pair of Chinese. "Now the prisoners must agree to my judgment." He addressed them. "Do you both abide by my decree? To leave the ranks of TRIO forever and to take that which you have stolen with you?"

"Dui!" the robbers chorused. To go free *and* to take the gold they had stolen was an incredible turn of good luck.

"Please forgive the shame we have brought upon ourselves and TRIO," one thief stated.

"We shall always regret betraying our brothers," said the other. "And we humbly submit to the sentence you have passed."

"I thought you would," Tosha Khan told them, then signaled to his muscular follower Wulanji, who exited the chamber. He returned seconds later bearing, by its curved wooden handles, a small cast-iron stove.

Wulanji set the stove at the base of the platform upon which Tosha Khan stood. Heat radiated from the stove's black interior. There were two containers positioned over its grill, with the steam from whatever was boiling inside them rising in a haze into the air.

Tosha Khan glared down at the thieves. "You are free to go. In anticipation that you would agree to my terms, I made the gold that you have stolen easier to carry." The Mongol warlord smiled and pointed to the containers bubbling on the stove. "Open your mouths, filth. And drink."

5

David McCarter emerged from the pay telephone stall at Manila International Airport and gave the rest of the Phoenix Force crew the good word.

"It's all set," McCarter informed them. "I found my mate's phone number listed in the directory. He says he'll be right over to give us a lift into the city. Said he shouldn't be more than thirty minutes, depending on the traffic."

"Did he ask how you happened to be in the Philippines?" Yakov Katzenelenbogen asked.

"Sure," the Briton answered. "I told him me and a few friends of mine decided to come over for holiday."

Gary Manning wiped his hand against the back of his sweaty neck. "Some holiday," the Canadian grumbled. "We're not even out of the terminal yet and already I'm dripping wet."

"It goes with the climate," Rafael Encizo pointed out with a grin. "When you holiday in hell, you're bound to be a little warm."

"Shit, this ain't warm," Calvin James concluded as they began carrying their gear to where they were going to meet McCarter's friend. "This here's the *cool* part of the day. It's not even lunchtime. Wait until after twelve, that's when this furnace is *really* gonna heat up."

Manning shook his head and muttered, "Wonderful."

Taking a commuter flight to Calvin James's old stomping ground of San Francisco, the men of Phoenix Force had caught Philippine Air Lines flight 101 without problem. Leaving the Bay Area at 10:30 Sunday night, their PAL 747 touched down on schedule in Manila at 7:30 A.M., Tuesday morning. With the exception of Katz, who always felt better when his feet were firmly planted on the ground, everyone pretty much enjoyed the flight.

As Hal Brognola had promised before their departure, none of the team's "luggage" had garnered any undue attention on either side of the Pacific. Passing through Philippine customs had entailed little more than showing local officials at the airport their passports. None of their equipment had faced an inspection.

In the time between their get-together with Brognola and leaving the U.S., no new information regarding the disappearance of the *Bruja del Mar* had turned up. The air-and-sea search that had been initiated after the ship first went missing was still going on, but at this stage was not expected to produce any positive results.

Having some of the Colombian ship's treasure show up in Manila for sale was still the best and only concrete lead they had.

Manila is served daily by some thirty international airlines representing the major cities of Asia, Australia, Europe, the Middle East and North America. Given the unbelievable congestion inside the terminal, it was easy to suspect that all of the international flights into Manila for that day had disembarked at the same time.

People of all ethnic origins crowded the main terminal through which Phoenix Force walked, making their progress slow. But McCarter was not to be bothered. In a short while he was going to be reunited with a very close friend of his, which meant that he could overlook the rest.

McCarter had not met his friend Mahmud until well into his second year of working undercover against Communist subversives in the Royal Colony of Hong Kong. Mahmud was of the Bajaus, sea gypsies of the Philippines, whose traditional home was to be found in the emerald-green seas off the Sulu Archipelago, the southernmost islands of the Philippines.

Mahmud had come to Hong Kong at the request of his sister. Her husband had lost his job as a taxi driver when his right foot was amputated as a result of a tragic automobile accident. What savings had been set aside quickly dwindled to nothing. No one wanted to hire the brother-in-law. Feeding a family of six was proving impossible.

To add to their misery, Mahmud's sister gave birth to the couple's fifth child, thereby straining to the breaking point an already shaky existence. To their horror, they came to realize that if the rest of the children were to survive, the burden of raising their newest child would have to be eliminated.

And so the baby had been sold, traded for a miserable sum of money that, ultimately, did little to ease the family's dire situation. Shortly thereafter, the taxi firm the father had worked for contacted him about a dispatcher's job that was available. The family rejoiced. With a steady source of income they could now afford to buy back the child they had sold.

Their delight at the pending reunion with their baby lasted as long as it took the parents to visit the "agency" that had purchased the child. They were too late. The infant, the stunned mother and father were told, was no longer in Hong Kong, but had been placed with a family in Thailand and could not be returned.

Heartbroken, the grieving parents went home. A week later Mahmud received a letter from his sister asking for his help. Mahmud arrived in Hong Kong three days later, but by then the adoption agency was nothing more than an abandoned storefront.

Mahmud took his sister's problem to the Hong Kong police where he summarily got the runaround until he happened to mention the name of the adoption agency. The next thing Mahmud knew, he was being ushered into the cramped closet McCarter used for an office.

McCarter took an immediate liking to the hearty Bajau man. For Mahmud, the feeling was mutual. McCarter revealed that the adoption agency had been under suspicion by the authorities for the past two months.

Linked somehow to a Communist drug-smuggling ring, the exact nature of the bogus agency's role in the operation was still under investigation when news arrived that the phony agency had closed up shop. McCarter promised to inform Mahmud as soon as further information became available.

But that solution was not suitable to the stubborn Bajau, who insisted that he be allowed to participate in the investigation. McCarter had always believed in listening to his instincts. Something told him bringing Mahmud in on the case was the right thing to do. Without having to second-guess the wisdom of his decision, McCarter accepted Mahmud's offer of help.

The grueling investigation into the Communist drug-smuggling ring lasted six months, but it was not until clues led to the Haadyai region in southern Thailand that the grisly truth behind the adoption agency's involvement in the operation came to light.

Babies purchased in Hong Kong were flown to Thailand where they were killed, emptied of all internal organs and then stuffed with bags of heroin. The bodies were then carried over the border into Malaysia as sleeping babes in the arms of their "mothers."

Only infants less than two years old were used in the scheme, so that their long periods of "sleep" seemed natural. Bodies were used within twelve hours of death while the faces still looked lifelike.

McCarter thought he had seen it all, but this stood out as one of the worst examples of cruelty he had ever come across. The smuggling operation was crushed and soon after the Briton's mission in Hong Kong was brought to a close. McCarter and Mahmud had parted company, keeping in touch over the ensuing years through the occasional letter or postcard.

And now he and his Bajau friend werc to be reunited. To the Londoner's knowledge, Mahmud had never revealed to his sister the monstrous fate of her child. McCarter would always admire the special courage of Mahmud's silence.

The five members of Phoenix Force made their way from the terminal to the spot where Mahmud said he would meet them. The outside air was humid and hot; it was like walking into an oven. The taste of rain and dirt filled the air. The distant clouds looked angry and mean.

"So what's this friend of yours like, David?" Manning ventured once they were outside. McCarter had told them little of Mahmud's background. "Is he anything like you?"

"What can I say?" the Briton said with a shrug. "Mahmud is tough, honest and he laughs at my jokes. Come to think of it, he reminds me of you, Gary."

Manning rolled his eyes.

"Decent of him to pick us up like this," Katz said. "It's always better when we can take advantage of someone local helping us out. It saves time and permits our moving about less conspicuously.''

The blaring sound of an automobile horn interrupted the Israeli, prompting Manning to comment, ''Don't count on it.''

Encizo indicated the lavishly decorated vehicle with the beeping horn that was edging through the traffic in their direction. ''That wouldn't be your friend, would it?''

McCarter looked and nodded. ''It's Mahmud on the hooter, all right. Grab your bags, gents.''

Manning muttered to Calvin James, ''*And* he laughs at McCarter's jokes.''

DANIEL DEMATTIA was not a stupid man.

His younger brother, who labored paddling office workers across the Pasig River in a company-owned *banca* dugout, was stupid. His older brother, with three illegitimate children and an aversion to using prophylactics, was stupid. And heaven help the dubious mental capabilities of his Uncle Robert, the only person, to Daniel's knowledge, to work more than twenty-five years unloading ships at the port of Manila without stealing a single article of value for himself or his family.

To Daniel DeMattia, a customs inspector stationed five days a week at Manila International Airport, a stupid man was a foolish man. And DeMattia was no fool. Especially when it came to picking up some easy extra cash. Which was precisely what he intended to do the second he saw how his superior, Galo Viratos, reacted to the arrival of the five passengers of flight 101 from San Francisco.

Daniel DeMattia knew something was up when Galo met the passengers in question and personally escorted the men through one side of the customs inspection sec-

tion to the other. Not a single one of the passengers'
many bags were examined, a sure sign to DeMattia that
a bribe had been paid.

Daniel did not mind that the foreigners were given the
VIP treatment. It happened all the time. What irked
DeMattia was that the offer of the bribe had not come to
him first. At the very least Galo Viratos could have invited him to share in his good fortune. But no. Daniel's
greedy pig of a boss had decided to hog all of the bribe
for himself, cutting Daniel out of the action altogether.

Fortunately, Daniel DeMattia had other options open
to him. He waited until the five people cleared customs,
then excused himself to place a phone call.

If the passengers were worth the special attention Galo
had given them, then perhaps they were also the kind of
people his contact at Metrocom paid him to be on the
lookout for.

Daniel DeMattia was betting they were.

6

Mahmud waited until introductions were made and they were rolling along Imelda Avenue away from the airport before he let out what could only be described as a whoop of pure delight.

"Oh!" Mahmud blinked, as though surprised by his own enthusiasm. "But you must excuse me, I am afraid. It is just the excitement of seeing you again, David. I know when we last saw each other during that unfortunate business in Hong Kong that we said we would someday meet again. I can only admit now that it has happened, that deep in my heart I doubted it ever would. How are you, my friend?"

McCarter answered, "Keeping match fit as usual."

Mahmud laughed. "Ha, ha! I see you still fancy yourself as the witty one. *Match fit,* that is pretty good!"

McCarter's face darkened momentarily as Manning was heard to comment from the back seat, "I like this guy's style."

Mahmud glanced at his English friend as they drove. "I am joking, of course, David. You are looking one hundred percent. Really, I must be frank with you." The Bajau lifted the lid of a Styrofoam cooler next to the driver's seat and pulled out a soft drink can that was resting on ice. "Still hooked on the cola?" He tossed the can of Coke to a grateful McCarter.

"You remembered, Mahmud." The Briton caught the can. "Cheers." McCarter had picked up the habit while stationed in Vietnam. He popped the tab on top of the can and guzzled a third of its contents. "Ah, that's better."

Mahmud motioned to the others. "Help yourself."

All but Katz took a drink from the cooler.

Mahmud waited a half minute for McCarter to finish his Coke, then said, "So, tell me, David. What is all this crap you were giving me on the telephone about popping into Manila for a vacation? Did you really expect me to believe your story?"

"I had my hopes," admitted McCarter.

"Feeble ones at best, my friend. In Hong Kong you had a talent for sniffing out trouble, or else trouble came looking for you. I do not think things have changed that much." Mahmud flicked his eyes to the rearview mirror. "And if I had any doubts, I need only take note of the men you travel with. You and they are of the same breed. Am I not right?"

"I'm really not at liberty to say, Mahmud."

The Bajau's eyes seemed to shine. "Good. You *are* here on business, then. That you would give me the call when you arrive tells me I may now be of help to you as you were once to me. How long do you plan to stay in the Philippines?"

"It all depends," said McCarter. "My friends and I are looking for something that's been stolen, and aren't too sure where to start looking."

"But you have an idea where to begin your search?"

"A company called Serrano's House of China." McCarter discarded the empty can of Coke and helped himself to another. "Ever hear of it?"

"Sure. It's a small business located in the Makati district, across the street from a car park at the corner of Rada and Dela Rosa. Fellow that owns the place is named Victor. I wouldn't trust him with my chickens. A real seedy character. Is he expecting you?"

"We kinda thought we'd drop in unannounced," Calvin James offered.

"Yeah," added Encizo. "If he knows we want to see him, he might go all shy on us."

"Or worse," Mahmud warned. "Victor Serrano has friends in low places, if you know what I mean. I am told he can be a really tough customer when he wants to. Then again, there are two sides to that coin, David. Yes?"

"Right, mate."

"In that case," Mahmud continued, "I would suggest you unpack your luggage as we drive and prepare yourselves with suitable attire. You never know in the Philippines when the climate is apt to change. It is best to be ready for the storm before it rains."

"The climate changes often here, does it?" Katzenelenbogen asked.

"Too much for some. Not enough for others," Mahmud noted. "Most countries have the secret police, you see. Many countries have *two* such factions at work. In the Philippines, though, it is our good fortune to have *three* secret police outfits to protect us. We have Metrocom—the Metropolitan Command Intelligence Division of the Philippines Constabulary. Their job is to eliminate enemies of the state."

"And the other two?" Encizo questioned.

"That would be ISAFP and NISA. The first is the Intelligence Service of the Armed Forces, while the second is our National Intelligence Security Authority. NISA watches over all the activities of the other two and keeps them in line.''

Mahmud frowned. ''If there is a chance your business here will attract *any* of the Philippine secret police, then you would do well to protect yourselves. Too many good people have disappeared.'' The wiry Bajau's voice hardened. ''They are the ones NISA or the rest take to 'salvaging.' One day they are here, then they are gone, not to be seen again until their bullet-riddled body turns up in the field, the forest or floating in the river. It would disappoint me to have your vacation end that way, David.''

''Advice taken,'' McCarter said, then turned to the rest of Phoenix Force. ''Mahmud's right. Now seems as good a time as any to bring out the hardware.'' He nodded to Encizo. ''You want to pass me my bag?''

The Cuban complied, and during the next few miles of highway all of the Phoenix Force members armed themselves according to individual preference.

''David has informed us that you are of the Bajaus,'' Katz said, trading the three-pronged prosthesis he favored for the less conspicuous artificial arm. The ''hand'' of the device contained a .22 Magnum single-shot pistol that could be fired by manipulating the muscles in the stump of his arm.

''Of Sitankai,'' Mahmud confirmed. ''You are familiar with my people?''

''Only what I've read in magazines,'' the Israeli confessed. ''But the articles led me to believe that all Bajaus were fishermen.''

''Most of us are,'' Mahmud said. ''I am what you would call an exception to the rule. The truth of the matter is that the life of living on a house of stilts above the water is not for me. Nor am I overly fond of sunsets on the Pacific or dodging pirates or smugglers.''

"Bollocks," McCarter said, laughing, then explained to Katz. "He gets seasick."

"Hey," Mahmud protested, "I was born with lungs, not with gills and fins."

"I understand," Katzenelenbogen told him. "I feel the same way about flying."

Mahmud smiled. "Same difference. Anyway, I get by just fine without having to fish for a living. When I am not driving out to Manila International Airport to pick up a dear and trusted friend, I am one of Manila's finest jeepney drivers." He affectionately patted the dashboard of the vehicle they were riding in. "Do you like it?"

"I always wondered what they did with all those props left over from *Star Wars*," Manning commented.

"Ha!" Mahmud laughed hard. "That is a good one! I am pleased to see that David has not cornered the market on good humor. 'Props from *Star Wars*,'" he repeated. "I like that!"

When Manning first saw Mahmud's jeepney, a lavishly decorated compilation of surplus U.S. Army jeep parts, an oversized body, glittering paint, chrome and reflectors, the Canadian's reaction was one of disbelief. To Manning, given the sensitive nature of their mission, riding around in such garish transportation was tantamount to advertising the presence of Phoenix Force in the Philippines.

The farther Mahmud drove them into the growing snarl of Manila's traffic, though, the more Manning's concerns on the subject evaporated. Everywhere he looked the multicolored jeepnies could be seen, zipping in and out of the mounting congestion of the capital's streets.

Mahmud took them over the South Superhighway and into Makati. They turned right at impressive Manila Garden Hotel, then headed up Pasay Road until they reached Paseo De Roxas. Several more blocks and one left turn later found them curbside across the street from their destination.

"There it is." Mahmud stopped his jeepney but kept the engine running. "Serrano's House of China. You want me to wait while you go inside?"

McCarter barked good-naturedly, "What do you think?"

"Just checking," the Englishman's friend replied. "I will be parked just down the street with my eyes glued to the front of the building. Never fear. If you need a ride in a hurry, Mahmud will be there to give it to you."

"Any idea what this Victor Serrano looks like?" James asked.

"I have seen his picture in the newspapers," Mahmud answered. "Serrano is short and stocky with black hair and plastic-rimmed glasses. From a distance he resembles an overgrown *lumpia*—the Filipino version of the Chinese eggroll."

"Thanks, Mahmud," an amused McCarter said, then he and the rest of Phoenix Force left the jeepney and crossed Dela Rosa to Serrano's place of business.

"How're we gonna handle this?" Calvin James wondered as they made their way across the street. "There's no reason for all of us to pump the guy for answers."

"Calvin's right," offered Encizo, then motioned to McCarter. "Why don't you and Katz do the honors? The rest of us can make like tourists in front of the place."

"Fine with me," McCarter agreed, by which time they were standing before the double glass doors leading into the House of China. "All Hal knew about this Serrano guy was that he'd been approached to purchase one or more items known to be part of the *Bruja del Mar*'s cargo. We don't know if his involvement goes beyond that."

"Let's see what Mr. Serrano has to say," suggested Katz, then he and McCarter pushed open the doors and entered.

The cool interior of Serrano's House of China reminded McCarter of a library—not because it was stacked floor to ceiling with shelves of books, but because of the vacuum of silence that greeted his ears.

"Business doesn't exactly appear to be booming," McCarter observed. As far as he could tell, he and Katz were alone.

Serrano's House of China featured a long row of display cases that ran in an L-shape in the center of the showroom floor. Inside the cases were numerous pieces of porcelain and pottery from the Ming, Tang and Sung dynasties. Adjacent to the protected display area were six pedestals, positioned at intervals of about three feet. Atop the pedestals were prize pieces of porcelain.

McCarter was not impressed. "All this space and this is how they use it? Some 'House of China.'" He indicated a piece of pottery resting upon one of the pedestals. "They oughtta call the bleedin' place 'House O' Jelly Jars'!"

"May I help you, gentlemen?" A voice sounding as though it could have belonged to an eggroll came at them as the owner of Serrano's House of China appeared through a doorway. "I see you have been admiring our display." His round eyes blinked behind the lenses of his plastic-rimmed glasses. "I am the Serrano of Serrano's House of China. How may I help you?"

By way of an explanation Katz lifted one of the antique jars from its pedestal and whistled to McCarter.

"Catch," Katz said, then sent the jar flying in a lazy arc through the air. McCarter waited until the last possible moment before deftly catching the jar with one hand.

"Gentlemen!" Serrano trembled with rage. "What is the meaning of this?"

McCarter balanced the base of the jar on the palm of his hand. "We want some answers, sunshine. And you're gonna give 'em to us."

"Are you mad?" Serrano demanded. "That is Ming Dynasty pottery from the fifteenth century!"

"Heads up!" The Phoenix Force unit commander whistled, sending another of the antique Chinese trade pottery pieces sailing in McCarter's direction.

"Hold on." McCarter gritted his teeth, snatching the second Ming treasure with his free hand. "Like I was saying, sunshine," the Briton reminded his stammering adversary, "I want some answers."

"What?" Serrano pleaded. "What knowledge do I possess that can possibly be worth the destruction of such beautiful artifacts?"

"Knowledge concerning a number of pre-Columbian artifacts that were presented to you for sale," Katz said as he walked to another pedestal. "We want to know what you know."

Serrano played dumb. "I have no idea what you are referring to."

"No?" Katz scooped the fingers of his left hand around another of the rare pottery pieces. "Are you absolutely sure about that?"

"Wait, wait!" Serrano's magnified eyes were rooted to the Ming treasure that was bobbing up and down on the

Israeli's open palm. "You can't be doing this. You men aren't even Filipino, so you can't be with the police."

"Start singing, Serrano," McCarter advised. "Or else my friend's gonna make me play catch again. Who knows? In all the excitement I may just drop everything!"

"No, no!" Serrano pulled an initialed handkerchief from the inside pocket of his coat and daubed his sweating brow. "It is as you say. I *was* approached to see if I was interested in purchasing several objects of pre-Columbian art."

"You saw the objects?" Katz asked.

"Only one, a single goblet. It was shown to me to whet my interest."

"And you verified its authenticity?" Katz wanted to know.

Serrano nodded. "The goblet was genuine. It belonged to El Dorado, called 'The Gilded One,' a king or priest of the Muisica Indians. It was his practice to be covered head to toe in gold dust, then wash it all off in Guatavita Lake in the Andes north of Bogotá."

"Good for him," McCarter said. "Those who brought this goblet to you, were they Filipino?"

"Yes, but I had never seen them before."

"How'd they know to come to you, then?" Katz quizzed.

"In certain circles I am known as a procurer of..." Serrano hesitated.

"Difficult to obtain objets d'art?" Katz supplied.

"That is one way of looking at it."

"In other words you're a middleman for stolen pieces of art." McCarter was not impressed. "So, back to this goblet. How many pieces were offered to you altogether?"

"Five," Serrano said. "And the asking price was most expensive."

Katzenelenbogen concluded, "But not so expensive that you couldn't turn a profit on a deal?"

"Correct."

"If that's the case," McCarter said, "then why haven't you purchased the objects yet?"

"As I explained, the price they were asking was quite high. I was only approached Sunday evening. I needed some time to raise the amount they were asking."

"Umm-hmm," McCarter said, "and now you're probably ready to make the buy."

Serrano sighed. "I am."

Katz was still bouncing the Ming pottery up and down in his hand. "When and where is the exchange to take place?"

Serrano swallowed, looking for a way out. He fingered the frames of his glasses and coughed, aware that his starched shirt collar was cutting into the back of his neck.

"You must understand, gentlemen," the Filipino fence pleaded. "If I reveal to you when and where the transaction is to take place, then in all likelihood the deal will not go through."

"And *you* must understand, sunshine," McCarter informed Serrano, "that unless you start talking, my mate here and I are gonna trash this place. Top to bottom. You got that?"

Serrano's shoulders sagged in defeat. "I understand. I was contacted by telephone earlier this morning. I am to take the money for purchasing the objects to the Hotel Intercontinental Manila this evening. The buy is to be made at nine-thirty tonight in room 726. I bring the cash.

They bring the art objects. I swear to you that is all I know."

"We believe you, Victor," McCarter assured the man. "'Cause if you're winding us up, we'll come back and level this place."

"A word to the wise, Mr. Serrano," Katz submitted. "Don't make that meeting tonight."

"I've already made other arrangements," Serrano assured the Israeli.

"Good," Katz said, then whistled to McCarter. "Catch."

The valuable Ming pottery piece went tumbling through the air to McCarter. The Briton considered his options, then casually tossed one of his centuries-old jars to Serrano. "Don't drop it."

McCarter carried his pieces of pottery over to Serrano and handed them to the shaking Filipino. "Good show, Victor. Not ready for amateur hour, but a good catch all the same." McCarter turned to Katz. "Shall we?"

"Yo!" Calvin James shouted as he pushed his way through the front door.

"Trouble?" Katz guessed.

"An update on the weather report," the Phoenix fighter confirmed. "We've got company!"

7

"How long have they been here?" Katz asked as he and McCarter followed Calvin James outside.

"Less than a minute," Calvin answered. "You think that Serrano dude triggered some kind of silent burglar alarm?"

McCarter shook his head. "Not that we saw. Maybe we were tailed from the airport."

"Possible," Katz concurred.

McCarter looked around. Mahmud was sitting behind the wheel of his jeepney, supposedly reading a newspaper, halfway up the block.

Separating Phoenix Force from Mahmud's position was a dark blue sedan. Six men filled the seats of the car front and back. The sedan had a twin, including the same number of passengers, parked against the curb on the opposite side of the street.

"I want to keep Mahmud out of the rough stuff if we can," McCarter said.

Calvin James, watching the driver of the first sedan speaking into a microphone, had other ideas. "We may not get the chance, David. I think they're getting ready to make their move."

A glance across Dela Rosa confirmed that the driver of the second sedan was also on the radio.

"We'll split up," Katz said. "We're too easy to pick off clumped together like this. David, you, Manning and Encizo head for the jeepney. Calvin and I will start up the street the way we came. Since they haven't moved in on us yet, maybe their orders are to keep a low profile and just watch what we're doing. If that's the case, then perhaps the three of you can make it to Mahmud okay."

"And after we make it to the jeepney," McCarter said, "Mahmud can swing by to give you and Calvin a lift."

"*If* we make it to the jeepney," Manning added.

Making a show of shaking hands as though they were saying goodbye to one another, the members of Phoenix Force separated according to plan. McCarter ignored the dark sedan and its passengers as he, Manning and Encizo walked by, apparently lost in the importance of a discussion they were having.

So far it looked good. They were better than two-thirds of the way home. Mahmud had put down his newspaper and was waiting for them to reach the jeepney. As McCarter ostensibly said something to Manning he could see from the corner of his eye that Calvin and Katz were doing all right, too. Another hundred feet or so and they would be in the clear.

"You there!" An amplified voice came at them through a bullhorn. "You three! Stop where you are!"

Instinctively the three Phoenix Force pros put some distance between themselves as they turned to the sound of the voice. The six men from the dark sedan were climbing from the car. The man who had been riding shotgun held a bullhorn to his lips. Across the street the men from the second sedan were also getting out.

"Now what?" Manning whispered.

McCarter grinned, a knot of excitement gripping his heart. "We improvise. Be ready."

McCarter broke away from Manning and Encizo and went straight toward the men from the dark blue sedan.

"Something I can help you fellas with?" the Briton asked in his strongest Cockney accent.

None of the six men moved. All were Filipinos of varying sizes and ages. Their basic uniform consisted of a two-piece leisure suit, with white shirt and thin black tie.

"We are with Metrocom!" the man with the bullhorn announced, then added, "You and your friends are under arrest! You will spread your arms and legs and lie facedown on the ground!"

"Piss off!" McCarter hollered in defiance. He spun on his heel and started back to Manning and Encizo.

"David!" Manning cried, his hand flying beneath his jacket for an Eagle .357 Magnum.

McCarter dived to the ground and rolled to the left. Gunfire erupted behind him. His fingers found the walnut grip of his Browning Hi-Power as Metrocom bullets ate chunks from the sidewalk at his feet.

Gary Manning shouted his warning to McCarter even as one of the six secret policemen prepared to gun the Briton in the back. McCarter was on the ground and out of the way when the barrel-chested Canadian's gun cleared leather.

The .357 in Manning's fist boomed twice, both blasts slamming hard into the trigger-happy hotshot who had tried to kill McCarter. One slug ripped through the target's belly just above the belt buckle, churning the man's bowels to bloody butter.

The next deadly egg from Manning's Eagle cracked the loser across the chin, instantly raising the dead-on-his-feet gunman's jawline by three full inches. The body collapsed to the street with a smack.

Encizo's Walther PPK was out of its shoulder rig a heartbeat after Manning had drawn his .357. The fearless Cuban leaped below the protection of a parked Volkswagen bus as the remaining five men from the first Metrocom staff car opened fire with an assortment of weapons. Glass shattered and punctured metal whined as enemy bullets Swiss-cheesed the VW.

"¡Mierda!" The Cuban flattened himself to the pavement, crawling along on his stomach. Slugs peppered the air overhead. As he scanned the area between the tires of the German car, Rafael saw that one Metrocom thug was sneaking up on him.

Encizo aimed his PPK and fired, the .380 round striking the man in the shank of his right leg. Bones snapped like dry kindling, jagged splinters from a fractured tibia jutting through flesh and fabric. Blood washed over the ragged piece of bone. The injured man dropped his .38 to the ground and sank to the street, clutching at his wound in a mad fit of pain.

Rafael let the Metrocom screamer thrash a little closer before putting him out of his misery with another dose of doom from the Walther. The .380 missile hit the Filipino in the neck, neatly severing the jugular vein and treating the side of the Volkswagen bus to an impromptu paint job.

McCarter came out of his roll, his Browning Hi-Power looking for blood. The Englishman smiled. The loud mouth shouting the orders had traded his bullhorn for an M-1 SMG. McCarter went after the subgunner before he had a chance to use it.

Rising to his feet and running to the right to avoid a fresh volley of Metrocom slugs, McCarter opened up with the Browning. Both of the Phoenix sharpshooter's shots connected with their intended objective.

The Thompson SMG clattered from the gunman's hands as twin 9mm bullets performed some Hi-Powered surgery on the Filipino's face. One disintegrated nose and a missing left eye convinced the man it was time to die.

From his vantage point behind the bullet-riddled VW bus, Encizo watched as the Metrocom crew from the second sedan hurried across Dela Rosa. The Cuban freedom fighter let the representatives from the hush-hush school of law enforcement get halfway to their goal before cutting across their flank with his PPK.

One of the Filipino flatfoots took a hit in the groin and went down in a bumpy skid. The Smith&Wesson Model 10 he had been carrying fell from his grasp and discharged when it hit the road, its .38 Special slug castrating the man next to him. Both sang the high-pitched praises of pain as they began bleeding to death.

The rest of the Metrocom honchos racing across Dela Rosa quickly regretted their decision. Shooting McCarter or Manning was impossible without running the risk of gunning down one of their own. Getting to Encizo was not any easier. Already the Cuban had reduced their number by two. He was protected by the Volkswagen bus, while out in the open their collective hides were up for grabs.

In mounting desperation the Metrocom second-stringers opted for the only logical course of action available. They executed a sloppily staged retreat and double-timed it back to their car.

Manning, McCarter and Encizo were still exchanging bullets with Metrocom survivors from the first sedan when the final two Phoenix Force hard liners joined the battle. Calvin James wielded his Colt Commander, while Katzenelenbogen tore into the Metrocomrades with his Beretta.

With James and Katz in on the fight, their Metrocom foes were caught in a cross fire. One of the government-sanctioned bullies threw away his empty pistol and made a play for the Thompson submachine gun at his feet. He was reaching for the tempting M-1 when a shot from Calvin's Colt opened the side of his rib cage to the elements. A follow-up shot from Manning finished the job by ripping the man's throat out. His dying momentum carried his leaking corpse forward and over the unused Thompson.

The Metrocom pair still in the fight were standing in the middle of hell and they knew it. Neither doubted they were going to die. Both were determined to kill at least one of the foreign devils any way they could.

Making the final mistake of his life by choosing Katz as the easiest of five possible targets, one Filipino madman left the relative sanctuary of the sedan he had been hiding behind and charged the Israeli. His gun firing blindly at what he considered to be a sure kill, and screaming at the top of his voice to intimidate his foe, the Metrocom assassin expected his gray-haired opponent with the paunchy waistline to cringe in fear.

Colonel Yakov Katzenelenbogen did not budge. Steeling himself to the Filipino's unorthodox charge, the Israeli met the wild assault by unleashing the power of his deadly Beretta.

Three shots thundered from the autoloader Katz held, all but one of the .380 hollowpoints plowing through flesh and bone. The Metrocom suicide jockey's eyes widened in shock as fire consumed his midsection and his legs stopped working. His free hand fumbled to ease his pain and came away with a stringy section of small intestine clinging to his fingers. He opened his mouth to cry and deflated with a dying whimper to the sidewalk.

McCarter's Browning officially ended the career of the final Metrocom bad guy with a knockout hit to the face. Blood obliterated the government cop's features and the gun he had been using bounced to the pavement. A second later the body did the same.

"Here comes our ride!" McCarter shouted to his Phoenix Force pals. Mahmud had the engine of his colorful jeepney racing and was speeding up Dela Rosa.

"Do we need correct change?" Manning asked as Mahmud's jeepney screeched to a halt.

"Better ask the cruds across the street," suggested Calvin James as he and Katz jumped into the jeepney.

A quick glimpse showed the four Metrocom gunmen from the second sedan regrouping for another attack.

"Not to fuss," Mahmud assured them as Manning, Encizo and finally, McCarter, leaped into the jeepney. "Leave the driving to us!"

The doors to the jeepney slammed shut. Mahmud mashed his foot to the accelerator and the vehicle lurched forward. Metrocom bullets pelted the air. One of the jeepney's reflectors exploded as it was hit.

"What the *kwan* did they do that for?" McCarter's Bajau friend fumed. Steering with his right hand, Mahmud's left hand suddenly appeared through his window—gripping a sawed-off shotgun.

"Oh shit!" James remarked.

Mahmud triggered the shotgun as they zoomed past the Metrocom enforcers. One of the undercover bulls caught the brunt of the blast and went down. Mahmud fired again, this time blowing away the left rear tire of the enemy's sedan. The rest of Metrocom's poorest scattered and ran.

"Like I said before," Mahmud reminded them as he brought the shotgun back inside, "it always pays to be ready for the sudden change in the weather!"

"No kidding?" McCarter indicated the shotgun across Mahmud's lap. "Love your taste in Auntie Ellas. Bloody diabolical!"

Mahmud laughed and sent the jeepney careering around a corner. "*Mabuhay!* Welcome to the Philippines!"

8

McCarter aimed his Ingram M-10 machine pistol at the flimsy wooden door. No one in the cramped quarters of the room uttered a sound. Everyone waited, mentally counting to ten. On ten the knocking started again. Three times, a pause, then twice. McCarter signaled to Manning.

"All right," the Briton instructed.

Manning eased open the lock on the door and moved to one side.

Still keeping his M-10 trained on the door, McCarter called out, "Whenever you're ready, mate!"

The knob on the door turned slowly and Mahmud stepped in out of the rain. In the Bajau's arms were a cardboard barrel of fried chicken and a plain white paper sack. Mahmud passed the chicken to Encizo, then crossed to a closet to hang up his coat.

"Sorry about the delay." He held the top of the paper bag in his mouth as he slipped the sleeves of his raincoat over a hanger. "She's pissing down like the banshee. We get rain all the time, but nobody knows how to drive in the stuff."

Encizo tore open the lid on the chicken container and everyone helped themselves to some food. The cooler from Mahmud's jeepney was stocked full of drinks and sat in one corner of the room.

"So, what'd you find out, Mahmud?" McCarter said as he selected a crispy chicken leg. "Are our guests still planning on meeting with Mr. Serrano tonight in room 726?"

"Better than that, I'm afraid," Mahmud said, taking his white paper sack and crossing to a sofa. "So abundant are Victor Serrano's friends that they also occupy the room next to 726. But that is not the half of it. I believe I have determined who it is Mr. Serrano is scheduled to meet."

"Who?" Katz asked.

Mahmud wrinkled his nose in distaste. "All the ones staying in those rooms at the Hotel Intercontinental Manila are Communists."

"Communists?" McCarter repeated. "Are you sure?"

"Pretty sure." Mahmud reached into the sack and retrieved what looked to be a hard-boiled egg. "I have a close friend who works at the hotel who would know. He tells me there are seven, maybe ten men staying in the rooms...all of them members of the New People's Army."

"The NPA?" Manning scratched his neck. "How do they fit in?"

"It doesn't figure they're the ones that hit the *Bruja del Mar*," Calvin James concluded. "Serrano said they probably had up to five pieces to sell. That's only a small fraction of what's missing."

"True," Katzenelenbogen agreed. "If the NPA *did* have access to the entire treasure, they wouldn't bother with Serrano. He's strictly small potatoes. Serrano couldn't hope to put himself in touch with enough money to foot the bill for the entire package."

Encizo shrugged. "So how did the NPA come across part of the *Bruja del Mar*'s cargo?"

"And so soon after the ship disappeared," McCarter added. "If the NPA didn't actually stage the heist, then maybe they're teamed somehow with the real criminals."

"And only cut themselves in for less than two percent of the gold? Not to mention the jewels?" Manning shook his head. "Even for Communists that's bad business."

Mahmud tapped his finger against the top of the egg, opening a small hole in its shell. "I know you are not at liberty to discuss all of the sensitive particulars," he said, "but might not the Communists settle for a small slice of pie if they were not on the scene when the whole pie came out of the oven?"

McCarter chuckled. "Mahmud's right. The NPA might not be aware the rest of the treasure exists."

"Which could indicate the Communists came across the gold objects they have...how?" Calvin James asked. "Part of some kind of payment?"

"It makes sense," Manning said. "Let's say the NPA was given what they were from the *Bruja del Mar* in lieu of cash. As payment for what, we don't know. That would tell us why they got in touch with Serrano. They'd need somebody like him to purchase what they were selling without attracting the wrong kind of attention."

"I'll buy it," agreed McCarter. "The NPA came into the goblets and what *after* the treasure was off the *Bruja del Mar*. That makes the New People's Army our only link with whoever really *did* hit the ship."

James clapped his hands together. "Swell. When we meet with the NPA tonight, we'll just ask them to tell us where they got the gold and that'll be it. I'm sure they'll be more than happy to divulge such privileged information. And if not...?" He let the alternative hang in the air. "We apply a little pressure."

"Here, here." McCarter lifted a can of Coca-Cola to his lips and drank. "And the more the merrier."

They had been camped in the tiny room at Motel Bomba since early that afternoon. Of the five Phoenix Force soldiers, only Katzenelenbogen had ventured outside their room, going with a pocketful of Philippine pesos to a pay telephone to place an international call to Hal Brognola.

The report the Israeli received over Stony Man's scrambled line was skimpy at best. The wreckage of the *Bruja del Mar* had yet to be found, and the U.S. military was scheduled to call off its search efforts within the next twenty-four hours. With the exception of the five golden objects Phoenix Force already knew about, no more of the Colombian ship's precious cargo had surfaced for sale.

The only lead Brognola could supply that might be of any significance to their mission was the news that various underground art dealers throughout the world had been tipped to an incredible auction in the works. Specifics were vague, other than that the auction would take place during the next two weeks.

Katz ended the conversation by informing Brognola of a "hot date" that had been set up for later in the evening, then said goodbye. By the time Katz returned to relay the details of his talk with Brognola, Mahmud had already left on his fact-finding tour to the Hotel Intercontinental Manila.

"What's the scuttle on the street, Mahmud?" McCarter asked. "Any reporcussions from our clash with Metrocom?"

"Not officially," the Bajau replied, dipping a thumb and index finger into the top of the egg and bringing out the shriveled brown remains of a birdlike creature. "It's practically unheard of for the Metrocom boys to get beat at their own game. Press coverage about such incidents being what they are in Manila, I don't think you're talking about exactly making the headlines."

Mahmud put a leathery wing into his mouth and chewed. "Even without media coverage the people know what happened, though. Especially those belonging to *barcadas*—you would call them 'street families.' Most have greeted the defeat of the otherwise invincible Metrocom gangsters with a sigh of satisfaction. The ones upset are the ones owing Metrocom favors. You can be sure that Metrocom would like a rematch with you."

"Is Metrocom likely to track us here to the Bomba?" questioned Encizo.

"Perhaps. The government's computer system at Camp Aguinaldo moves slowly. It will be at least two days before a national bulletin has been issued with your descriptions. Even if Metrocom does learn about this motel, by then you will be somewhere else. If need be there are many such LABAN stations that would be happy to take you in."

Calvin James looked up from his food. "LABAN?"

"A sometimes militant political group dedicated to the overthrow of the present Filipino government," Mahmud said.

Thinking of the sawed-off shotgun his Bajau friend had used earlier in the day, McCarter commented, "You wouldn't be a member of LABAN, would you?"

Mahmud grinned and closed his mouth over the rest of the thing he was eating, then picked his teeth clean with miniature claws attached to one of the bones in his hand.

"Like you, David," Mahmud explained, "I am not at liberty to discuss all the details. I *will* say not everyone in the Philippines is content with the corrupt management of our beloved country. For years those in opposition have tried to affect reform at the ballot box, but when the government is voting with torture, bullets and bodies, even the best of intentions reach a breaking point. Many of my acquaintances believe the water has already boiled over the edge of the kettle."

The Briton nodded his head in understanding. "Say no more, mate. I read you loud and clear." McCarter had always respected Mahmud's judgment and saw no reason not to do so now. "I've been meaning to ask, Mahmud."

"What's that, David?"

"I noticed you weren't having any chicken. There's plenty for everyone, you know."

The Bajau showed McCarter the pile of tiny bones in his hand. "That's okay. I've been eating my *balut*."

McCarter grimaced. *"Balut?"*

"Semifermented duck egg, six weeks old." Mahmud reached into the white paper sack in front of him. "I have another *balut* in the bag if any of you want to try one."

"Maybe next time," McCarter said, declining. "If you don't mind, I think I'll stick to the fried chicken."

So did everyone else.

9

McCarter flicked the last of his Player's cigarette into a puddle. A nasty habit, he thought, remembering how he had once heard smoking defined as a fire at one end and a fool at the other. One of these days he would quit.

The drive to Makati Commercial Center from the Ermita district took Mahmud and his jeepney less than half an hour. If the day-long rain had dampened the spirits of Filipinos living in Manila, the Phoenix Force squad saw nothing about the city's bustling nightlife to indicate this.

The Ermita district, where the Bomba Motel was located, was particularly lively. Situated two short blocks from the bay-front grounds of the U.S. embassy, the district served as a cornerstone for any number of businesses catering to human vices.

If it involved sex, drugs or alcohol, Mahmud explained as they drove along, Ermita district was the place to find it. In some parts of the area prostitutes outnumbered pedestrians. Blue-uniformed "security cops" stood guard at the doors of sex clubs to haggle with customers. Harsh neon signs over the clubs flashed out lewd messages in a rainbow of colors. Explicit posters decorated outside walls of seedy bars. Every sexual taste was depicted.

Drugs were sold like candy in the district. Besides marijuana from Thailand, exotics such as Bagulo Gold and

Mogadon were readily available for sale. A stiff wind would have created a snowstorm of cocaine.

Mahmud had parked his jeepney opposite the enclosed flight of stairs leading from the ground to the top floor of the Hotel Intercontinental Manila. One of the largest hotels in Manila, the fourteen-story Intercontinental featured 420 rooms and every luxury imaginable. The glass doors leading to the stairwell were not locked. The majority of guests staying at the Intercontinental preferred using the hotel's elevators, so more often than not, the stairwell was deserted.

McCarter pulled his raincoat closer about his body as Manning and Encizo joined him outside the jeepney. Rather than have everyone from Phoenix Force participate in the meeting Victor Serrano had arranged with the NPA Reds, Calvin James and Katz were to remain downstairs.

Past experience had taught the Stony Man superpros that nothing about a given operation was ever one hundred percent predictable. Unexpected variables inevitably cropped up. Not being prepared when they did could easily mean the difference between a long life and a premature grave.

"Lovely weather," Manning commented, cool rainwater trickling down his neck as he stepped from the jeepney.

"What do you expect, amigo?" Encizo wondered with a smile. "You're bound to suffer a little discomfort when you travel in the off-season."

McCarter checked his watch. They still had twelve minutes before the scheduled meeting with the NPA. Taking the stairs to the seventh floor would consume a third of that time. The Englishman poked his head back into the jeepney.

"We should be back by nine forty-five," he told Katz and Calvin James. "Any longer than that and you'll know the meet's spoiled."

"If you're not down by then," Katzenelenbogen promised, "you'll see us upstairs."

To which Calvin James added, "Watch your ass up there, huh?"

"Damn well better believe it," McCarter said, trading a final glance with Mahmud, then turning to Manning and Encizo. "Shall we?"

"Anything to get out of this rain," the big Canadian responded.

Together the three Phoenix Force warriors walked the short distance to the Intercontinental's stairwell, their ankle-length raincoats serving a greater purpose than mere protection from the inclement weather. Each of the men was armed to the teeth. Hopefully the raincoats would conceal that fact from anyone they might pass on their way upstairs.

McCarter's Browning Hi-Power rode ready and waiting for action in shoulder leather. He also carried an Ingram M-10 machine pistol with sound suppressor, hung by a strap against his right side. Two SAS concussion grenades and a pair of M-26 fragmentation blasters rested in various pockets.

Gary Manning preferred rifles to handguns, but when his weapon of choice was out of the question he favored the long range and reliable knockdown power of a Magnum handgun. As he had earlier in the day, the Canadian was once again using an Eagle .357 Magnum pistol.

The Phoenix Force demo expert's pockets were packed with grenades and ammo. He also carried four ounces of C-4 plastic explosives—just in case they needed to blast their way out of trouble.

Rafael Encizo was no slouch in the weapon department, either. The Cuban was prepared to clash with trouble with the best of them. Besides the Smith&Wesson M-59 autoloader worn on his hip, Encizo's hardware for the foray into the Intercontinental consisted of a silenced Heckler&Koch MP-5 machine pistol, which Encizo carried on a shoulder strap.

As expected, the stairwell remained deserted for the duration of their climb. Nor did they encounter anyone when they abandoned the stairway for the plush carpeted corridor of the seventh floor. For all they could tell they were the only ones in the hotel.

Suits me, McCarter decided as they started down the hall for rooms where the NPA sales reps were staying. Fewer people out in the open lessened the risk of innocents being caught in the middle if the meeting with the Communists went sour.

Pilipino is the national language of the Philippines and one of three official languages; English and Spanish are the other two. Since none of the three spoke Pilipino, and speaking English would have tipped the NPA off immediately that Victor Serrano was not going to show for the meeting, having Encizo go the Spanish route was the logical alternative. He had the honor of first approaching the NPA gold merchants.

They moved around a bend in the corridor and stopped. Directly ahead was room 726. Next to it, number 728. According to the information Mahmud had obtained, both rooms accommodated NPA Communists. Farther down the hallway a set of two elevators faced each other.

McCarter moved silently past the first NPA room and proceeded along the corridor until he was opposite and to the side of the next door up. He slipped his hands over his silenced M-10 and nodded to Encizo that he was ready.

Manning removed the Eagle .357 from its holster and pressed himself against the wall next to room 726.

Then Rafael pivoted and went to work, beating his left fist upon the door, while simultaneously shouting to the occupants inside.

"*¡Fuego!*" Encizo cried in alarm. "*¡Fuego! Todos afuera! Salgase del edificio!*"

The Cuban stopped knocking and stepped two paces back, waiting to see if the threat of fire in the hotel was enough to bring the NPA out of their hole. No sooner had he moved away than he had his answer. The door was thrown open and a gun-toting Filipino nervously poked his nose into the hallway.

"*¡Minchione!*" the wild-eyed Red rasped, fumbling to bring his Czech Vz-25 submachine gun into play. The slow-on-the-draw Communist should have spent his last seconds on Earth making funeral arrangements.

Throwing open his raincoat, Encizo withdrew the MP-5, cutting loose with the unleashed fury of his weapon, hosing down his intended target with a sputtering 9mm parabellum shower. The Red danced around in the doorway on invisible strings, the front of his white cotton shirt sprouting fountains of blood. With trembling lips his life left his body and the Vz-25 dropped to the carpeted floor.

"*Ramon!*" a male voice screamed from inside the room, and someone tried slamming the door shut. It made it as far as the corpse blocking the entry, then stopped. "*¡A la chingada!*"

Encizo traced a crisscross pattern over the middle of the half-closed door and was rewarded for his efforts by a grunting gasp of surprise on the other side. The door quit trying to close and the thump of a body falling to the floor reached the Cuban's ears.

Manning motioned to Rafael. "Let's crash the party."

Encizo agreed completely. Crouching, he charged the door, butting it hard with his right shoulder, throwing the door back on its hinges with a loud crash. The Cuban pushed into the room, sweeping the business end of his Heckler&Koch from left to right.

A startled NPA hardcase was diving for a Winchester 97 shotgun on a coffee table. The acrobatic Communist managed to brush his fingers over the Winchester's walnut stock before Encizo's MP-5 lifted him into the air. The ranks of the New People's Army were reduced by one as the dead man left a smearing signature of blood upon the wall.

His sixth sense warning that someone was behind him, Encizo leaped swiftly to the side as the chatter of enemy bullets devoured the carpet near his feet. Tufts of the flooring reached for the sky. Rafael responded to the attack by bringing his MP-5 around for the kill.

Gary Manning was already there.

Twice the Canadian's Eagle boomed, filling the room with thunder. Manning's aim was true. The Communist gunning for Encizo stopped a pair of .357 blitzers the hard way. One shot tunneled through the guy's chest and exploded out his back in a hole as big as a softball. The follow-up strike from the Magnum shredded the skinny Filipino's face to a disfigured mess.

"*¡Gracias!*" Encizo called, then turned to confront a couple of lunatics wielding M-3 SMGs racing from a bedroom.

Orange flame belched from the barrels of the grease guns as the NPA duo opened fire, the enterprising killers dividing their attention between Manning and the Cuban. The door next to Manning's head rained sawdust on his shoulder as it was peppered with a flurry of .45 slugs. The coffee table by Encizo was reduced to firewood.

The Communists blazing away with the M-3s suddenly realized they had blown their opportunity to eliminate Encizo and Manning. That burst of brilliance registered on their feeble brains the instant the Cuban and the barrel-chested Canadian began firing back.

The first subgunner lost all fervor for the cause when a storm from Manning's .357 transformed his stomach and liver from functioning internal organs to mangled pieces of dying tissue. Another shot deposited a Magnum-sized kidney stone in the last place it belonged. The man's agonized scream died the same time he did.

The Communist squaring off with Encizo didn't fare any better. The Filipino revolutionary was bringing his burping M-3 to bear on the Cuban when he made the fatal mistake of catching three 9mm slugs from Encizo's MP-5 in his mouth. Shattered teeth, bits of ragged tongue and a severed uvula became the condemned Red's last meal. His head snapped to the ceiling. Eyes glazed over in death as the body sagged to the floor.

No sooner had Encizo and Manning vanished into room 726 when the door to 728 suddenly snapped open. The NPA soldier running to the aid of his comrades was so intent on getting next door that he failed to notice McCarter on the opposite side of the hallway.

Stupid geezer, McCarter decided, then whistled to get the Communist's attention. "Over here!"

Phil Becerra reacted to the sound of McCarter's voice with a gasp of pure astonishment, but that was not half the surprise he experienced when the owner of that British accent began pelting his body with bullets from a silenced submachine gun.

As the first of many slugs from the M-10 began puncturing his flesh, Becerra forgot all about helping his cohorts next door. Poor Phil Becerra had worries of his own—like how to keep his heart beating after most of it had been gored from his chest. Becerra's solution to the problem was to wait and see what happened. It was a short wait.

GEAR UP FOR ADVENTURE SWEEPSTAKES

Gold Eagle® Announces 1985's Most Exciting Sweepstakes. You May Win An American Motors Jeep® CJ Off-Road Adventure. Only In A Jeep.®

Take a look at what you can WIN!

Grand Prize 1986
American Motors Jeep

Second Prize 10 Pairs
of Binoculars

Third Prize 100 Pairs of
Gold Eagle Sunglasses

Grand Prize: 1986 American Motors Jeep® CJ
(Retail Value $8,500.00 U.S.)

Second Prize: 10 Pairs of Binoculars
(Retail Value $90.00 U.S.)

Third Prize: 100 Pairs of Gold Eagle Sunglasses
(Retail Value $6.95 U.S.)

The Action doesn't stop here!

Four Novels And A Rugged Digital Watch **FREE**

That's what you'll get free when you take this opportunity to sign up with the elite corps of Gold Eagle Home Subscribers.

Here's seven great reasons why you should become a Gold Eagle subscriber:

- 16% saving off retail price
- 6 new titles every other month
  (2 Mack Bolan® and one each of Phoenix Force®
  Able Team® Track™ and S.O.B.'s™)
- Books hot off the presses
- FREE delivery and handling
- FREE Automag newsletter with every shipment
- Eligibility to receive special books at deep discount prices
- Cancellation privilege at any time

Rush Your Order To Us Today

Don't let this bargain get away. Send for your four free books and watch, now. They're yours to keep even if you never buy another Gold Eagle book.

Double Barrelled Excitement

Use the card below to enter the Gold Eagle 'Gear Up For Adventure Sweepstakes.' You can also use this card to become a member of the Gold Eagle Subscriber corps.

Official Entry Form
WIN a 1986 AMC Jeep® CJ

Please check one:

☐ Yeah, enter me in the **Gold Eagle Gear Up For Adventure Sweepstakes** and send me four **FREE** Gold Eagle novels plus my free digital quartz watch. Then send me 6 brand new Gold Eagle novels every second month as they come off the presses. Bill me at the low price of $1.95 each (for a total of $11.70 per shipment, a saving of $2.30 off the retail price). There are no shipping, handling or other hidden charges. I understand that these 4 books and watch are mine FREE with NO obligation to buy

☐ No I don't want to receive the four FREE Gold Eagle novels and digital watch. However, I DO wish to enter the sweepstakes. Please notify me if I win.

166 CIM PAGP

Name:_____

Address:_____ Apt:_____

City:_____

State:_____ Zip:_____

Subscription Offer limited to one per household and not valid for present subscribers. Prices subject to change. See back of book for rules and regulations.

A division of
WORLDWIDE LIBRARY ®

GOLD
EAGLE

'Gear Up For Adventure Sweepstakes'
Win a 1986 AMC Jeep® CJ
Off-road adventure — Only in a Jeep.®

Detach, Affix Postage and Mail Today!

Gold Eagle
Gear Up For Adventure Sweepstakes

P.O. Box 797,
Cooper Station
New York, New York
10276

Put stamp here.
The Post Office
will not
deliver mail
without postage.

McCarter cautiously regarded the half-open door his victim exited. Furniture was visible beyond the perimeter of the doorway. Nothing else. No more of the NPA Communists emerged. It made sense that the others would learn from one dead man's error in judgment.

For all McCarter could tell, room 728 could be teeming with NPA. The Phoenix Force sharpshooter wanted to find out one way or the other, but *not* by putting his neck in a noose. With gunfire tearing from the room 726, McCarter fed his left hand into the pocket of his raincoat and brought out an M-26 grenade.

Gripping the steel body of the lemon-shaped bomb, the Briton pulled the safety pin and tossed the olive-drab grenade through the open doorway into room 728. He jumped to the side of the door and dropped to one knee just as the M-26 exploded, shaking the wall against which his shoulder was braced and abruptly rocking the flooring beneath his knee like a miniature earthquake.

The noise from the explosion was still dying down when another, far more satisfying sound replaced it—the moans and groans of wounded NPA Reds.

"Sweets for the suite," McCarter observed, pleased with himself. Rising from his crouched position, his Ingram at the ready, the Phoenix commando forced himself into the grenade-blasted room.

Smoke and plaster were everywhere. A crater in the floor provided a glimpse of the room below. The M-26 had taken out at least two of the NPA radicals. One headless torso rested a few feet from the bedroom door. There was no sign of the head it was missing. A second body bled profusely onto the carpet from a dozen oozing wounds, any one of which would have been fatal.

"Ohhhh," came a soft cry from behind the front door. McCarter whirled to take out his opponent, stopping only

short of killing his foe when he realized the Communist was
flat on the floor and barely conscious.

Keeping his weapon trained on the man, the Briton slowly
approached, getting halfway to the stricken Communist
when the sensation of a wet breeze came at him from behind. In a blinding blur McCarter spun on his heel, dropping low, his M-10 erupting to life as a series of anxious .45s
chopped at the air over his head.

The Phoenix Force fighter gritted his teeth in anger, letting his powerful machine pistol reach out and touch the
Communist who had been hiding on the balcony outside the
room. The NPA assassin was gunning for McCarter with a
Thompson Model 1921, but might as well have stuck to a
slingshot for all the good the subgun did him.

With less than fifteen feet separating him from his target, McCarter ran the Ingram's magazine dry. Hot 9mm
slugs punched into the Communist, sledge-hammering his
jerking body into a backward spill through the open sliding glass door and over the rail of the balcony.

"Drop in again some time, pal," McCarter said as he
stood and quickly swapped magazines on the M-10.

DOWNSTAIRS IN MAHMUD'S JEEPNEY, Yakov and James
were staring intently at the Intercontinental when the
screaming body of the airborne NPA man came hurtling
earthward. The shrieking lasted as long as it took the Communist to plant himself headfirst into a flower bed.

"I think," Katz said, reaching for the door of the jeepney, "that someone we know on the seventh floor has just
rang for room service."

Calvin James nodded grimly. "Let's go see what they
want."

10

"It is the Metrocom!" Mahmud's alarmed exclamation shook the interior of the jeepney.

"Who the fuck invited them?" Calvin James wondered, watching with Katz and Mahmud as four Metrocom sedans pulled into the parking lot of the Hotel Intercontinental Manila like separate sections of the same black metal snake. The clock on the jeepney's dash had yet to reach nine-thirty. "You think they were called about the trouble upstairs?"

"I doubt it," Katz answered. "David and the others have not been gone long enough for a response to have been made."

"What then?" asked James.

The doors of the Metrocom sedans popped open in unison and a small army of Filipino secret police poured out into the rainswept night.

"My money says we were sold out by Victor Serrano," the Israeli concluded.

"If that's the case he's a no good bastard!" Mahmud swore.

"We left survivors during our confrontation with Metrocom earlier today," Katz said. "It's reasonable to assume that they had a chat with Serrano after we were gone."

"And he bought his ass off the hot seat by telling Metrocom about the meeting he tipped us to." James would have loved nothing more than to have Serrano sitting with them in the jeepney right then. "Shit! How many of the dudes are there?"

"I count twenty," replied Katz, "five from each car."

"Looks like they don't intend on getting their butts whipped twice in one day," the black Phoenix warrior stated. The plainclothes thugs boldly brandished an assortment of weapons, including automatic rifles, pistols, shotguns and SMGs.

Mahmud's jeepney was virtually ignored as the secret police of Metrocom streamed by, hurrying across the parking lot for the glass doors at the bottom of the Intercontinental's stairwell. Seeing the legs of the NPA reject sticking out of the flower bed only spurred the cops to greater speed. They were on to something hot and they knew it.

A pair of Metrocomers made it to the glass doors and opened them up for their buddies. Two-thirds of the group continued on through a door at the base of the stairwell, while the remaining five men began taking the steps two at a time.

"The larger bunch is going for the elevators," Mahmud said.

"And the rest are going up the way we did," added James, "which will pin McCarter, Encizo and Manning smack dab in the middle."

Katz nodded and nudged his partner. "Come on. I feel like a climb."

"Want me to come, too?" Mahmud volunteered.

Katz shook his head. "Not this time. It's better for us if you stay down here. Turn your jeepney around and back into the parking space. Keep your engine running.

We may need a fast ride back to the Bomba before this is over.''

The Israeli opened the door of the jeepney and he and Calvin James jumped out.

"Good luck!" Mahmud called.

Katz slammed the door and they were on their way to the stairwell, running across the rain-slick pavement of the Intercontinental's parking lot.

"There's no way we can stop the bunch in the elevators from reaching the seventh floor," Katzenelenbogen said as they ran. "They're probably already on their way up."

"So we go for the five in the stairwell," James suggested in response. "Metrocom ain't the only ones that can play the sandwich game."

MANNING AND ENCIZO completed their inspection of the NPA outpost just as McCarter's M-26 grenade dropped in on the room next door. The resulting explosion shook the floor beneath their feet and knocked an oil painting off the wall.

"Sounds like David's having fun," remarked Manning, a belief confirmed a few moments later when the chopping rumble of a machine gun reached their ears.

"He's enjoying himself, all right," said Encizo.

Room 726 had not produced any NPA holdouts. All the Communists on tap when Manning and Encizo first entered were now sitting front row center. Of the five pre-Columbian art objects Victor Serrano had been negotiating to buy, only three of the items had actually been found—the goblet Serrano had mentioned, plus a pair of what resembled oversized golden hat pins.

"That's it," Manning offered when their inspection was finished. "Time to go. If the police aren't already on their way to investigate all the shooting, they soon will be. I'd like us to be long gone before they get here.''

"Coming through!" McCarter announced loud and clear, then stepped into the room, the unconscious body of an NPA Communist draped over his left shoulder.

"Look what the cat dragged in," Encizo observed.

"He followed me home," McCarter supplied. "Can I keep him?"

Manning surveyed the carnage strewn about the room. "Guess we'll have to. Nobody else is left. How come he's still breathing?"

"Slipping up in my old age," McCarter explained. "He must've been crouching in the corner behind the door when I fragged the room. He's grazed on the forehead, but he'll live. At least long enough for us to have a little chat with him." The Englishman hefted the unconscious man higher on his shoulder. "Let's make tracks before I decide he's too heavy."

Manning motioned with his thumb. "What's it look like in the hallway?"

"Bare," McCarter answered. "Even if there are other guests staying on this floor, they're keeping a low profile."

Manning holstered his .357 and hurriedly crossed to the remnants of the coffee table where he retrieved the Winchester 97. "This may come in handy." He checked to make sure the shotgun was loaded. "Let's go."

With the Canadian leading the way the Phoenix Force soldiers exited the room, Manning ascertaining that the hallway was indeed clear before signaling for his friends to follow. Instead of heading right and to the stairwell, Manning went left.

"The elevator?" Encizo questioned as they rushed along.

"It'll be faster," Manning replied. "We can ride it as far as the second floor, *then* go for the stairwell."

McCarter grunted under the weight of his NPA burden. "Sounds like a winning combination."

They reached the elevators and Manning pushed the down button, waiting less than fifteen seconds before a musical chime played and the doors to their left began to open.

"That was fast," Manning said.

"¡Hideputa!" Encizo swore.

The elevator doors opened completely and the Phoenix Force tigers found themselves face-to-face with more than a half dozen Metrocom secret police.

Judging from the assorted weapons the legalized hoods carried, they were expecting plenty of trouble. The shock registered on their startled faces, however, made it plain that they were far from prepared to deal with the realities of a heated confrontation quite so soon.

Gary Manning *was* prepared. His reflexes honed to perfection through years in the field and under enemy fire, the burly Canadian flew into action, bringing the might of the awesome Winchester 97 to bear on the Metrocom cops.

The 12-gauge had no disconnector, which meant that Manning could hold the trigger back with his finger and pump the shotgun to his heart's content, firing each time the slide was cycled. In less than four seconds he had drained the gun of its seven shots.

Putting the fearsome trench broom through its paces was a delight for Manning, but it was much less a thrill for the Metrocom thugs huddled together inside the elevator. Each time the Canadian fired, nine pellets, each over .30-caliber in diameter, rocketed into the elevator.

The man nearest the blast was practically decapitated, the top of his skull shaved to an inch above his upper lip. The two behind him grappling for their guns were ventilated with through-and-through shots that rendered their vulnerable insides to bloody mush.

Another Metrocom moron saved his government a fortune in pension payments by having his rib cage reduced to a series of bony spokes protruding from his chest.

The final three targets the Winchester 97 eliminated literally died without knowing what hit them, splattering the interior of the stylish elevator with blood, torn bits of scalp and generous chunks of brain tissue. Their bodies slumped to the floor in a pile, joining the others.

The doors to the elevator silently closed as the car was summoned to the hotel's lobby.

"So much for the elevator. *And* the Winchester." Manning tossed away the empty shotgun and brought out his Eagle. "Guess it's the stairway after all."

"If we can still use the stairs," McCarter grumbled, carrying the deadweight of the grenade-dazed Communist and starting down the corridor toward the stairwell.

They were almost to the bend in the hallway when they heard the musical chime of the floor's second elevator go off.

Encizo, who brought up the rear, turned to the sound as eight more Metrocom troopers spilled into view.

"Better speed it up, guys!" the Cuban directed.

The first Metrocomer off the elevator spotted the retreating Phoenix Force trio and their unconscious prisoner immediately, his round face breaking into a triumphant smile as he separated from the rest of his fellow officers and began to give chase.

"You there! Halt!" he shouted. "You are all under arrest!"

He raised his revolver and fired twice, both shots from the .38 drilling neat side by side holes in the wall by Encizo's head.

"Rafael?" a concerned Manning called over his shoulder.

"I've got him," came the Cuban's terse reply.

Encizo dropped to one knee and unleashed his H&K MP-5 on his advancing foe. The silenced German submachine gun jerked in his grip, lacing the Metrocom gunman back and forth across the thighs, opening the target's belly in a bright bubbling fountain of gore.

The target's legs wobbled under the strain of too much to do and not enough life left to do it. He gritted his teeth as burning pain filled his universe and tumbled in a sloppy skid to the carpeted floorway.

Encizo cut loose with a short burst of 9mm fire at the remaining clump of Metrocom madmen, then sped around the bend in the hallway after his friends. Manning was at the door to the stairwell, holding it open for McCarter and their NPA prisoner.

"We'd better fly down the stairs!" Encizo yelled as he reached his companions.

"Stubborn bastards, aren't they?" commented Manning.

"Stubborn enough," Encizo agreed. "After you."

Manning nodded and ducked into the stairwell. Rafael waited for the first of the charging men from Metrocom to round the corner in the hallway. As soon as they did, the stocky Cuban put his MP-5 to work, blipping one enemy crud into oblivion, and sending the others backstepping for cover.

Satisfied, Encizo spun on his heels and disappeared into the stairwell. Manning and McCarter were halfway down to the sixth floor when Encizo caught up.

"I want to hear you killed 'em all," McCarter said wistfully.

"*¿Esta loco?*" the Cuban demanded. "I bought us twenty seconds, if that!"

"Just checking," McCarter returned, going past the sixth-floor level and continuing down to the fifth. He had scarcely managed to descend half a dozen steps when a series of shots rang out from below. "Son of a bitch!"

McCarter wheeled on the stairs and struggled back up to the sixth floor, Metrocom bullets eating the steps at his heels as fast as he could climb.

"When it rains it pours," said Encizo.

"Can we quote you on that?" Manning asked.

Out of curiosity the Canadian opened the door leading onto the sixth floor a fraction of an inch. More secret police were creeping down the hallway in the direction of the stairwell.

"They're on this floor, too," Manning said.

"So we're surrounded." McCarter lowered the body of the unconscious NPA Communist to the sixth-floor landing. "End of the ride for this one, I'm afraid. I try and pack-animal it out of here toting him on my back and that's all she wrote. Next month, someone else rents my flat."

Manning and Encizo knew McCarter was right. Attempting to fight their way out of the Intercontinental *and* take the prisoner with them presented too much of a liability to their safety.

"Leave him," Manning said. "It can't be helped."

Encizo peered over the cement edge of the stairway, catching a partial glimpse of the lead Metrocom hit man slinking up the stairs. Rafael took aim with his H&K and fired; bullets from the MP-5 dug baby fist-sized holes out of the wall of the stairwell, but left the Cuban's target unscathed.

At the first sign of danger the fleet Filipino beat a swift path downstairs and out of range. Encizo kept his eyes trained on the stairs in case the Metrocom soldier changed his mind.

McCarter jerked his thumb at the door going to the sixth floor. "How many out there?"

Manning whispered, "Three that I saw. Two skinny guys and a fat one. Ten yards down."

McCarter withdrew another M-26 grenade from his pocket. "I'll scratch 'em. Open the door when I say go."

Manning motioned with the Eagle. "I'll distract them with this."

The Englishman removed the grenade's safety pin with a twisting-pulling motion, then signaled to Manning. "Now!"

Manning tore open the door and began firing his .357, sufficiently unnerving the Metrocom sneaks inside the sixth-floor corridor for McCarter to launch the lemon-shaped bomb.

McCarter executed a sharp snap of his wrist, and the deadly M-26 rolled off his fingertips and soared through the air. The perfect pitch landed the grenade with a bounce in the middle of the group of secret police.

One Metrocom cop screamed helplessly as Manning closed the door with a slam and the M-26 exploded, shredding the men in the hallway in a bloody meat grinder of shrapnel and death.

Encizo glanced upstairs, aware that the door to the seventh-floor landing was opening. "Here they come."

McCarter readied his Browning Hi-Power. "Last time I stay in this bleedin' dump," he promised. "Worst case of overbooking I've seen. Even the stairwell's crowded."

Manning risked a glimpse beyond the door to the sixth floor. Instantly the edge of the doorframe was shattered with a spray of enemy bullets. Manning jumped back and allowed the door to close on its own.

"It's nice to feel wanted," the Canadian said.

A gleam shone from McCarter's eyes. "You ever wonder how we get into these messes?"

But before Manning could reply all kinds of hell broke out on the landing of the floor below. It started with a storm of automatic gunfire—the stuttering cough of an Uzi SMG interspersed with the reverberating thunder of a Colt Commander .45—and culminated with the feverish cries of the wounded and dying.

"You waiting for an invitation?" a familiar voice shouted up to them.

"It's Calvin and Katz!" Encizo hollered, starting down the stairs with Manning and McCarter right behind. Above them, leather-soled shoes pounded the steps as the Metrocom bunch on the seventh floor charged after their quarry.

Encizo and the others stepped over the bodies of five dead policemen as the complete Phoenix Force team was reunited.

"What took you so long?" McCarter protested.

"Bitch, bitch, bitch," Calvin James complained, leading the race downstairs. "Everything was cool till one of the NPA got kicked off the building. That you, David?"

"Who else?" Manning responded.

"Thought so," said James.

A wild shot came from behind and ricocheted around the interior of the stairwell.

"Any more Metrocom below?" asked Encizo.

The Phoenix Force squad was taking the steps two and three at a time, the distance between them and their pursuers growing by the second.

"They all went upstairs," Calvin answered.

"What about our ride?" Manning wanted to know.

"Ready and waiting," Katz finally spoke up, the team's elder member running up behind Calvin James.

"Finally," Manning said as they rounded the landing on the third floor and continued down to the second. "A piece of good news."

But all David McCarter could think about was the NPA prisoner they had been forced to abandon.

11

Major Carlos Cortega, regional commander of the New People's Army, sat on the stone slab outside the ruins of the Spanish fortress and waited. He was annoyed. He had expected to be admitted at once when he had explained to the guards why he wanted to speak to the Japanese. Instead, he had been told to sit on the slab of stone and wait until he was called for.

Cortega was perturbed. At forty-five years of age, the tall, straight-backed Filipino was used to inspiring a great deal more respect than those occupying the fortress seemed willing to give. What good was being a Communist if those who should know better failed to respect your station in life?

Major Cortega chewed at his fingernails. The past year had not been kind to the NPA, he reflected. Sure, with the government troops often poorly supplied and corrupted by involvement in local gambling and protection rackets, it was natural to expect the New People's Army to gain a stronger foothold in the Philippines. The Filipino people were sick to death, and sometimes even *put* to death, of the government that was supposed to be there to serve and protect them.

Ambushes during the past twelve months had increased by fifty percent. Where the NPA once limited attacks to a few soldiers isolated on patrol, the stepped-up campaign had Cortega and his Marxists boldly going after military groups of as many as fifteen men. Casualties among Cortega's men during such ambushes were rare, not too surprising since the brave soldiers of the New People's Army rarely attacked anyone unless the numerical odds were roughly ten to one in their favor.

Northern Luzon, the Eastern Visayas and Mindanao had all supported a marked increase in insurgent activities over the past year. Cortega's role in the scheme of things had resulted in the elimination of approximately seventy-five government troops, with more than double that number of local civilians killed.

While he truly regretted having to murder peasants to further the cause of the New People's Army, Cortega wisely understood that any substantial cultural advancement always involved personal sacrifice. That the ultimate price for this progress was usually paid by innocent men, women and children did not bother Major Carlos Cortega in the least.

In the past the NPA had enjoyed an immunity of sorts because most Filipino officials considered the New People's Army as nothing more than an anarchic band of ten to twelve thousand rebels led by a ragtag assortment of commanders. That bureaucratic blunder ended overnight with the seizure in the Visayas of secret NPA documents detailing plans for a multifront offensive and the establishment of a revolutionary government.

Once the contents of the documents were made public, the NPA's gravy train quickly derailed. Now, every one of consequence appeared to have the New People's Army on their hit list. Make that *shit* list, Cortega amended. Where he and his followers previously had virtual free run of the Filipino countryside, now they were forced to hide out in the forests like common criminals on the run from the law.

Carlos Cortega and his band of men had spent the past six months fighting to regain lost ground, but it had not been easy. More than forty thousand troops, nearly a quarter of the entire Philippine armed forces, were now stationed in the area centering around the Davao Gulf on the southern Philippine island of Mindanao.

Mindanao had traditionally served as a New People's Army stronghold, but no more. With the concentration of government troop strength at an all time high, Cortega and those like him had seen their sphere of influence drastically reduced. Like it or not, and Cortega did not like it, the mountainous regions above Mindanao's Davao City were now home to him and the NPA factions under his command.

Loyal though he was to the Marxist cause, Cortega had seriously toyed with the idea of packing it all in and getting into a line of work that would provide a finer standard of living than he was being forced to endure. Having financed NPA ventures through extortion, marijuana sales and stealing from the military, Carlos had not overlooked the security of his own economic future.

Whenever possible, Cortega had siphoned off some of the cream for himself; these were the rewards of being a leader, he liked to think. Over the years he had skimmed enough cash off the top to set himself up in business almost anywhere in the free world. If he ever did hang up his NPA hat, it would not be to face an existence of miserable poverty.

Cortega was preparing to put his plan of financial independence into motion when he was unexpectedly contacted by an emissary from TRIO. The Communist major had no idea what TRIO was all about. TRIO's business in the Philippines did not concern him. What *did* interest Carlos was that TRIO offered to pay him in gold for the rental of the old Spanish fortress located in the mountains of Mindanao within the "jurisdiction" of Cortega's New People's Army.

The prospect of renting the Spanish citadel to TRIO intrigued Cortega for a variety of reasons. Since the property was not being used anyway, turning a quick profit on the deal was too good an opportunity to miss.

Another aspect of the proposal Cortega appreciated was TRIO's insistence that all payments to the NPA be made in gold; not just *any* gold, but gold that would be worth many times its actual weight to buyers of the precious metal.

Major Carlos Cortega had long prided himself on his ability to drive a hard bargain. His business with TRIO was no exception. After TRIO's representative foolishly let slip that TRIO possessed twenty pre-Columbian gold art objects from which the rental for the fort was to be taken, Cortega informed the emissary that TRIO could have full use of the fortress for half of the treasure in payment.

The emissary grew indignant and balked at the price, much as Cortega knew he would. Counter offers were made, none of which were acceptable for Cortega's purposes or those of the New People's Army. Negotiations lasted for the better part of a day, and when they were finally brought to a close, an extremely satisfied Major Cortega emerged victorious.

Haggling with TRIO was like stealing candy from a baby for Cortega. He had told them he wanted half of their treasure, but in the end had settled for only a quarter. Twenty-five percent of the treasure was what Cortega had been shooting for all along, and because he understood the subtleties of driving hard bargains, TRIO had paid dearly for the privilege of doing business with Carlos Cortega.

Payment in full was made to Cortega the same day TRIO took up lodgings in the ruins of the mountain fortress. Cortega was elated and immediately set about arranging for the transfer of the art objects to Manila where they could be sold.

Eleven of his most trusted aides had accompanied the gold north to conduct the sale. By now his men should have returned. By now they should all be celebrating the joys of easy profit. By now Cortega should have siphoned even more of the cream to his burgeoning bankroll. But none of these things had happened. Something in Manila had gone terribly wrong.

Which was why Major Carlos Cortega was waiting to see the Japanese.

"He will see you now," the voice said.

Cortega jumped in his seat. So lost had he been in the depths of his own concern that he was unaware of the guard's approach. The NPA major composed himself and stood, then followed as the guard led him into the fortress and down a narrow corridor that eventually opened into a vast chamber of rough-hewn stone. A platform was erected at one end of the room, and it was on this dais that the Japanese sat.

"Why had you come here?" Sadatoshi Matsuno asked. Seated comfortably in one of the three undraped throne chairs, Matsuno regarded Carlos Cortega with amusement. The stupid NPA major had rented the facilities of the Spanish fortress to TRIO for next to nothing. The Communist was a clown and an idiot when it came to negotiations. Matsuno wanted to laugh.

"I have come about the gold that your people paid to mine for use of this citadel," Cortega said.

Matsuno smirked. "It's a bit late to be crying for additional payment. We agreed to your price and we paid it."

Cortega appeared insulted. "I have not come to quibble over what TRIO did or didn't pay the New People's Army," he confessed, "but to discuss a serious breech of security that could affect all of us."

The Japanese *yakuza* warrior nodded. "I'm listening."

"Eleven of my men went to Manila for the purposes of selling the objects of gold that we received from you."

"And how does that affect the sanctity of TRIO?"

"Something went wrong with the sale. All but one of my men were killed."

Sadatoshi's jaw tensed. In the absence of TRIO's three warlord leaders, who had departed Mindanao with an entourage of more than twenty warriors to conduct business elsewhere, he had been left in charge. Matsuno would see to it that their faith in him was justified.

"Who killed your men?" Matsuno asked. "Was it the police?"

Cortega shook his head. "Foreigners killed them and captured the gold we hoped to sell. One of my men lives, though, and it is because of him I have come to you. Metrocom has him."

The Japanese nodded. He was not unfamiliar with the various branches of the Filipino secret police, nor of the methods they employed to extract information from prisoners.

"And because your man knows what he does," suggested Sadatoshi, "it is reasonable to assume that Metrocom could learn of the arrangement TRIO has entered into with the New People's Army."

"Precisely," Cortega hastened to add, "why I came to you. I believe such a disclosure would not support the best interests of our respective organizations. While I am unaware of the full extent of TRIO's influence, I feel confident in surmising that you have access to certain individuals who could be most helpful to both TRIO and the NPA at this time."

"Perhaps," Matsuno said. "What would you have TRIO do, if it was within our power?"

"I have a close contact in Manila who knows much of the comings and goings of Metrocom and the rest. By one o'clock this afternoon I will know where my associate will be taken and when his interrogation is scheduled. I propose to pass this information on to you once it becomes available to me."

"At which point TRIO does what, Major Cortega? Effect an elaborate rescue mission for your imprisoned comrade?"

"No," Cortega answered. "Through his apprehension by Metrocom the integrity of the New People's Army has been compromised."

"You are speaking of a liquidation, then," Matsuno concluded.

"If possible, yes. I shudder to think what the secret police may discover if they are allowed to conduct business as usual."

Sadatoshi Matsuno stood. "Return to me when you have heard from your contact in Manila."

"Excellent." Cortega's relief was evident. "I am pleased TRIO will help with this problem."

"No," the proud Japanese *yakuza* corrected, "TRIO will not *help* with your problem. TRIO will *solve* it."

12

"It was a right cock-up," David McCarter bitterly complained. "We had that NPA geezer in the palm of our hands, and I had to go and leave him all trussed up for Metrocom."

"That's not how it was and you know it," Encizo said. "The guy was a liability we couldn't afford at the time; it's as simple as that. We never would have escaped with him along for the ride. He was excess baggage."

"Besides," Manning added, "just because Metrocom has him doesn't mean they're gonna get to keep him. What goes around comes around."

McCarter grumbled, "I don't give sweet f.a. about karma. The Communist we left for the secret police was our only link to whoever hit the *Bruja del Mar*. He was our key to the missing treasure. Once he starts singing to the coppers, we can kiss the gold and the jewels adios."

"It ain't necessarily so, man," Calvin James countered. "Mahmud said his connections with LABAN would do all they can to help us out. After stomping Metrocom's ass yesterday afternoon and again last night, we sorta qualify as heroes to half the people of this city. If there's a way for them to find out what Metrocom's plans are for the NPA prisoner, then we're going to find out, too."

McCarter sat down his can of Coca-Cola unfinished, a sure indication of just how upset he was. "I hear you talkin', mate, and I know what you're saying is true. It's just that *I'm* the one who had the prisoner, and *I'm* the one who let him go." He lit up a Player's cigarette. "Tell you one thing, though. I get my hands on him again it's gonna stay that way."

Katzenelenbogen checked the time on his watch. It was four o'clock on Wednesday afternoon, their second day in the Philippines. Phoenix Force had been cooped up in their room at the Bomba Motel since the previous evening. Inside the room it was muggy and hot, the same as it was outside.

It had been raining off and on for the past six hours, and so far the only bright spot of the day was an article Katz read in the morning newspaper announcing the arrest of Victor Serrano for unspecified "subversive activities" against the Filipino government. Evidently Metrocom's gratitude at being tipped off to the meeting at the Intercontinental was short-lived. Serrano would have done better keeping his big mouth shut.

Mahmud rapped on the door with a knock that identified him to his Phoenix Force friends. McCarter crossed to let him in.

"Well?" McCarter closed the door after Mahmud and followed his friend into the room. "I doubt you're wearing that silly grin 'cause you heard a tasty joke you want to share. What have you got?"

Mahmud pulled a chilled beer from the cooler in the corner of the room and twisted off the cap. "Good news and bad news."

"But not so bad that you can't smile about it," Katz suggested.

"It's as you say." Mahmud took a drink of the beer. "There is one hell of a tight lid on this Communist prisoner Metrocom caught last night. Everybody *knows* about him but doesn't know about him, if you see what I mean. He's under lock without the key."

"But you found out where he is?" guessed Manning.

"No," Mahmud confessed.

"I hope that's the bad news," McCarter said.

Again Mahmud shook his head. "No, that is not the bad news, nor the good news for that matter. Despite my many contacts, I have been unable to determine where the NPA prisoner is being held."

"Crap." McCarter frowned and crushed his cigarette in an ashtray.

"I could not determine where the captive is," the Bajau continued, "but I did learn where he will be taken for interrogation later tonight. And *that's* the good news."

McCarter relaxed and a broad smile spread across the vulpine features of his face. "I never doubted for a second you could do it, Mahmud. Cheers."

"Not so fast."

McCarter's smile did a slow fade. "Don't do this to me, Mahmud. What's the bad news?"

"Metrocom doesn't have the NPA prisoner anymore."

"Who does?" Katz inquired

"The National Intelligence Security Authority," Mahmud replied.

"Damn!" McCarter swore.

Mahmud nodded. "My feelings exactly. Unlike Metrocom and ISAFP, who are the *action* arms of the secret police, NISA is considered to be the *brains*—limited though they may be—of the Philippine security services. They have control over Metrocom and have obviously exercised that power by seizing the NPA prisoner."

"And I imagine," Encizo concluded, "NISA's just as adept at extracting information as Metrocom?"

"If anything," Mahmud revealed, "NISA is better. For all branches of the Philippine secret police, torture is part and parcel of a good day's work. Everyone is trained to do it; indeed, some of our highest ranked secret police studied at the International Police Academy in Washington before it was closed down.

"If NISA has its unfettered way with the NPA captive, then sooner or later they will bleed his soul dry of all they want to know."

"Which is what we're going to try and prevent," Gary Manning said. "Where is NISA taking the Communist for interrogation?"

"To a tobacco warehouse outside of Manila where NISA has set up a 'production room,' a place for torture. If you would reclaim the NPA Communist, then it is to this warehouse you must go. NISA and the prisoner should be getting well acquainted by eleven this evening."

Katz rose from his chair. "Thank you, Mahmud. You and your LABAN contacts have performed remarkably well."

"Does that mean you plan on visiting NISA at the tobacco warehouse tonight?"

"That's right," McCarter told his friend. "And if NISA gives us any trouble...we may just have to smoke 'em."

13

Daniel DeMattia was not pleased. For the second day in a row he was being cheated out of a bribe. For the second day running Galo Viratos, Daniel's greedy slug of a boss, had accepted a bribe that should have been shared by all. Or at least by Daniel. What kind of poor example was the chief customs inspector at Manila International Airport trying to set, anyway? Whatever happened to share and share alike?

The latest bone of contention DeMattia had to pick with his superior concerned certain passengers on the nine-thirty flight from Hong Kong. Members of a touring sports team, Galo had commented to DeMattia before sweeping to the opposite end of the customs inspection area to greet the "team."

Some team, DeMattia thought. He had been a sports fan for years and had never seen a so-called team like this one. There were eighteen of them, all roughly between twenty and thirty years old, with the kind of unfriendly faces nightmares were made of. Each was attired in a similar outfit of black trousers and jacket, with a black sweat shirt underneath. A uniform of sorts.

None of the visitors spoke unless addressed first by Galo, and when they did respond to Galo's comments, it was in short direct sentences. DeMattia had watched enough TV in his off-time to recognize hardened criminals when he saw them. And if he had any doubts about the "team's" true vocation, these were quickly dispelled once DeMattia got a closer look at the uninspected bags of "sports equipment" Inspector Galo Viratos whisked through customs.

Each of the Hong Kong visitors carried a single piece of luggage. Several of the pieces were sufficiently large to transport a few golf clubs, perhaps, but most were not much bigger than a shaving kit. Was that any way for a legitimate sports team to travel? The eighteen men from Hong Kong were in Manila to play a game all right, but not one that required season tickets or referees.

So Galo was letting the team through without a hitch, and Daniel's avaricious ass of a boss was pocketing another juicy bribe. What else was new? Once again Daniel DeMattia was left out in the cold.

Daniel entertained alerting his contact at Metrocom about the bogus team's arrival but decided not to. He was still waiting to receive payment for the information he had supplied Tuesday morning regarding the five mysterious passengers from San Francisco. More than twenty-four hours had passed and still no money. What did his Metrocom contact think Daniel was? A charity organization? No way!

DeMattia may have been annoyed, but he didn't raise a word of protest. What could he do? Galo was the one calling the shots. Nor did Daniel inform his Metrocom contact of the team's arrival as he could have done. If he was going to tip off Metrocom whenever something odd was up, then he was damn well going to be paid promptly!

Which is what Daniel was thinking as the Hong Kong visitors cleared customs and disappeared into the airport terminal nearby. Some touring sports team: six Chinese, six Japanese and six Mongolians.

DeMattia shrugged and vaguely wondered who the team had come to play.

THE FIVE PHOENIX FORCE WARRIORS silently followed the downhill path in single file. Beginning at the edge of the two-lane road where they had left Mahmud and his colorful jeepney, they had been on the narrow dirt trail for more than ten minutes.

Overhead, the late-summer nighttime sky was choking with clouds, all but obliterating the moon. Illumination was scarce. Mosquitoes fell across the path like hungry curtains. The taste of another rainstorm was in the air.

Working as pointman, Gary Manning signaled for the rest of the Stony Man brigade to halt as the path opened onto a flat barren field approximately fifty yards across. At the opposite end of the field the faint outline of a warehouse-sized building was visible.

The building was a storage facility owned and operated by the Tabacadera Tobacco Company and, if Mahmud's sources were correct, also housed a "production room," one of the special torture chambers used by the NISA secret police. A vehicle that reminded Manning of a bread delivery truck was parked in front of the building.

Next to the truck were a couple of four-door sedans. Two guards were leaning against one of the cars, passing time with cigarettes and conversation. The guards' easy manner made it clear that they were not expecting trouble.

"Piece of cake," Calvin James whispered to Manning as he joined the Canadian. "All we've got to do is ease our way across the open field without being seen, take out the guards and then duck inside the building to rescue the prisoner.''

Manning frowned and suggested, ''You're beginning to sound like McCarter.''

''I heard that,'' McCarter said, keeping to the cover of trees and vegetation growing along the edge of the field. ''What's the story?''

Calvin James indicated the guards standing watch. ''Looks like Frik and Frak are holding down the fort outside, while their pals go once around the block with the prisoner.''

''So, what's the problem?'' McCarter asked. ''All you gotta do is zonk both guards with the Anschütz. We scoot over to the warehouse, reclaim our prisoner, then we're on our merry way back home. Nothing to it. Piece of cake.''

Manning gave James a ''see what I mean?'' kind of look as Encizo and Katz joined them to assess their situation. No sooner had the Israeli and the Cuban settled down for an eyeballing of the tobacco warehouse when a second set of guards emerged from the building and traded places with the first.

''They're taking turns,'' Katz observed.

''A regular pack of Jimmy Durantes,'' James noted.

''Right, mate,'' McCarter agreed. ''Everybody wants into the act.'' He turned to Manning. ''How are they close-up?''

''Let's find out,'' Manning returned.

The Canadian sharpshooter lowered himself into a prone position and looked through the infrared scope attached to the Anschütz. One of the finest air guns in the world, the Anschütz boasted a range of more than a hundred yards.

Firing steel darts powered by a CO_2 cartridge, the air gun could tranquilize or silently dispose of the opposition with maximum efficiency and a minimum of noise. Outfitted with its infrared scope, similar to a Starlite scanner, which Manning had attached to the weapon to improve accuracy, the Anschütz was a sniper's dream come true.

Manning aimed the Anschütz at the guards in front of the warehouse. Both targets were clearly visible through the NOD scope that could take any available light, such as moonlight or starlight, and amplify it up to sixty thousand times. The end result from Manning's point of view was that the guards appeared through the scanner as though they were performing on a miniature television screen.

The first guard jumped to the hood of the nearest sedan and sat down, then pulled what might have been a bag of candy from his pocket. He offered his partner some of whatever the bag contained and, after his associate declined, laughed and eagerly attacked the sack on his own.

The Filipino secret cop's fingers were still lost inside the bag when the smile on his face suddenly showed too many teeth. His eyes rolled upward in surprise, then his body deflated backward onto the hood.

Unsure what had happened, Manning swept the nightscope to cover the second guard. As the NISA agent glanced over his shoulder to see what was wrong with his friend, his face suddenly sprouted a pair of pointed metal disks. Before his hands could pull the disks free, the guard's legs buckled and he collapsed to the ground.

Calvin James dropped to Manning's side. ''Good shooting, man, but I didn't hear you plunk those dudes!''

Manning's eyes never left the NOD. "That's 'cause I didn't."

The NISA guards had only been dead a few seconds before a swarm of black-clad assassins materialized out of nowhere beside the unmarked panel truck. The Canadian's gut tightened in a knot. He had seen such silent assassins before.

Manning pulled back from the air gun's scanner and climbed to his feet. "We've got party crashers. More than a dozen."

From where Phoenix Force was standing at the edge of the field, the black-clad killers were no more than shadows seeping into the warehouse building.

"They have to be here for the same reason we are." Katz stated aloud what the rest were thinking.

"Bloody hell to that noise!" McCarter grumbled. "I've already lost the NPA prisoner once this week. Not again!"

"I never cared for sloppy seconds, either," Encizo commented.

McCarter growled, gripping his M-10 tightly in his hands, "Let's do it, then. It's time for a punch-up!"

14

The prisoner's screams were music to José Despira's ears, a melody the NISA torture specialist never tired of hearing. It had been more than a month since José had entertained himself with a prisoner, far too long an interval.

There was nothing quite like a production-room session to stimulate the overweight Filipino's senses. Even sex ranked a pale second compared to the elation José experienced when doing what he did best. To completely have at his disposal the life and death of another human being was the most exquisite feeling in the world.

The interior of this NISA production room measured twenty feet square and was located in the northwest corner of the Tabacadera Tobacco Company's warehouse. A single bare lightbulb hanging from the center of the ceiling illuminated the room.

While most interrogations took place at night, the production room had been soundproofed to accommodate heavier schedules when a series of prisoners needed to be questioned on a round the clock basis. It was a proved fact that a gun could be fired from within the confined chambers of the room without alerting any of the warehouse's daytime workers.

Despira's guest for the evening was named Eduardo Ayala; the fat NISA thug had learned that much. Ayala was a Communist and a member of the revolutionary

New People's Army—information that Ayala had freely provided at the start of the questioning to, José suspected, hopefully avoid having to endure any torture later on.

If the ignorant Ayala was under the impression that cooperation up front would somehow let him off the hook, Despira saw no value in correcting that misconception. Let the Communist pig sing until his throat bled. Despira was not to be troubled.

Once Eduardo Ayala talked and divulged the information Despira wanted—and the NPA dog *would* talk— then Ayala's fate was in Despira's hands. Since the stinking Communist had already been deemed eminently fit for "salvaging" by Despira's superiors, he would slowly be tortured to death—to Despira's satisfaction—after he confessed.

Standing behind Despira were two of his subordinates, Rocha and Luna. It was their job to step in and lend a hand should Despira become fatigued in his duties. Two more of his men were killing time outside the tobacco warehouse for the same reason; somewhat of a waste of time considering that Despira *never* quit with a prisoner until he was finished with him or her.

Not that the NISA agent minded having an audience. As long as they stayed out of his way and gave him plenty of room to operate, José Despira enjoyed showing his associates how a master interrogator worked.

Despira waited for Eduardo's cries to fade to whimpers, then calmly spoke to the prisoner. "Ah, my friend. What can I say? You're not even trying. Not at all. I know you can scream louder than that. And so do you. Let's try it again. Hmmm?"

José Despira reached out with the portable electric

shock baton and lowered the end of the prod onto Ayala's bare stomach. Naked and tied on his back to a metal bed frame, the prisoner had been doused with ice-cold water to further add to his misery.

Eduardo Ayala waited helplessly for his tormentor to activate the prod and send a fresh wave of current rushing through his system. The bound man's chest rose and fell, his heart pounding like a kettledrum. His eyes danced in their sockets, watching in horror as Despira's thumb toyed with the control button in the middle of the prod.

Despira's pudgy thumb abruptly depressed the button and Ayala's stomach muscles surrendered to a paroxysm of pain. The man's body lifted in an agonizing arch, thrashing back and forth, scooting the legs of the bed frame across the floor.

Eduardo opened his mouth to scream, his vocal cords straining to the level of their endurance. His eyes bulged outward. He bit away the tip of his tongue and spit the pink morsel from his mouth. Blood from the wound stained his teeth a sticky red.

And then came the scream, wrenched from Ayala's throat like the cry of a wild beast. José Despira had been right. Eduardo *could* scream louder. *Much* louder. Why, if José Despira wanted him to, Eduardo was certain he could scream forever. He was certain he could....

Someone turned out the light in the production room.

"Ah, that's better."

Eduardo Ayala regained consciousness and was dimly aware that Despira's fat fingers were gripping his jaw.

"I'm so pleased you didn't decide to leave us," Despira said. "We have so much to talk about. You have so much to share."

Despira pulled down on Ayala's lower jaw, forcing the Communist's mouth open. The NISA torturer held a grisly piece of raw meat over the gaping target. "Silly boy. You bit off the end of your tongue. That's no good. Can't talk to me if you don't have your tongue."

José's fingers separated and the small chunk of flesh fell into Ayala's mouth. Despira smacked the heel of his palm against Eduardo's chin. The teeth met in a grinding crunch. Ayala started to choke.

The NISA sadist knelt down so his sweating face was less than an inch from his captive's. "Swallow it, scum! Swallow it or I'll hit you with the shock baton again. Swallow it!"

Ayala gagged and felt bile rising to the back of his throat, but he did as his tormentor ordered. He swallowed the jagged bit of tongue José Despira had dropped in his mouth.

"Excellent, Eduardo." Despira stepped away from the metal bed frame to which Ayala was manacled. "Now, I believe, we have established an open line of communication. I believe you are prepared to tell me everything I wish to know. Is that not true?"

Ayala's body sagged into the springs stretched across the bed and he slowly moved his head up and down.

"Excellent, excellent!" José Despira clapped his hands together. "Now, in a few moments I want you to begin telling me about the gold you and your friends were trying to sell to Victor Serrano. I want you to tell me where you got the gold and who the men were that attacked you at the Hotel Intercontinental last night. You think about these things and in a minute or so I'm going to let you tell me everything you know. All right?"

Again, the defeated Eduardo nodded.

José Despira smiled and turned to Rocha and Luna. "As you can see, gentlemen…Mr. Ayala is ready to talk to us. Be so kind, if you would, to go and fetch Tomas and Andal. I am sure they will find this pig's confession interesting."

"I'll get them," Rocha volunteered, then crossed to and opened the production room's thick padded door. "Be right back."

Rocha stepped into the warehouse and the padded door closed behind him.

"Good work as usual, José," Luna complimented his boss. "I personally didn't expect our boy to crack quite so fast."

"Nothing to it," Despira admitted. "These New People's Army filth are all alike. I've never worked on one of them who knew how to handle pain."

The padded door to the production room burst open and Rocha stumbled in, a great geyser of blood spurting from a severed jugular. He gurgled out an unintelligible warning, then slipped in a wet puddle at his feet and went down.

Despira and Luna were still reeling from the shock of Rocha's entrance when another unwelcome surprise charged into the room a pair of Chinese assassins clothed head-to-toe in black.

Desperately Luna fumbled for his revolver, pulling it free from its holster as the first of the Oriental killers attacked, yanking a four-pointed death star from a leather pouch at his waist and hurling it at the gun-toting NISA man.

Luna cried out as the throwing star struck him in the chest and sank inches deep into his pectoralis major muscle. The revolver in Luna's hand fired and the first Chinese was hit, the bullet cutting across the killer's right leg, opening the femoral artery in a wound that would eventually bleed the man to death.

But the gun-shot assassin was far from finished with Luna. Even as he toppled to the floor, the wounded Chinese unleashed another two death stars. Luna shrieked and fell to his knees in a writhing heap, one star stabbing into the deltoid of his right arm, another piercing his skull at the bridge of his nose. His revolver slipped from his trembling fingers and Luna died.

José Despira depressed the control button on the electric shock baton and leaped forward, covering only half the distance between him and his remaining adversary when the second Chinese assassin sent a crescent-shaped sickle blade flying in Despira's direction.

The fat Filipino gasped as the blade bit through the flesh and bone of his wrist. The Chinese killer drew back on the chain the sickle was attached to and pulled hard. The electric cattle prod José held clattered to the floor, a heartbeat ahead of Despira's right hand.

The NISA torturer clamped his left hand over the bleeding stump at the end of his right arm and screamed, amazed in his delirium to discover that not only NPA Communists had trouble handling pain.

15

David McCarter reached the front of the tobacco warehouse seconds ahead of the rest of Phoenix Force. The corner of the structure featured a sloping entryway leading into the building. The entrance was sufficiently high and wide to permit the transfer of goods in and out of the warehouse.

McCarter paused, pressing against the sturdy wooden frame of the entryway, staring into the inky darkness within the building, listening for any indication of the shadowy figures who disappeared inside. There was nothing. The interior of the warehouse was lost in a veil of murky grays and blacks.

The Englishman glanced behind as Manning and the others joined him, everyone relieved to have made it that far without drawing attention to their presence. Manning had left the Anschutz air gun hidden at the edge of the field and was armed with his .357 Eagle.

"Any sign of 'em?" Manning's question was scarcely audible.

"Not in that muck," McCarter replied. "Too dark. We have to have some light. Otherwise, it's suicide."

The high-pitched scream of a male voice came at them from somewhere inside the warehouse.

"Time to move," McCarter whispered to his Canadian friend.

And before Manning could comment one way or another, McCarter was gone, slipping around the edge of the entrance and vanishing into the building.

"Otherwise, it's suicide," Manning muttered to himself.

The British Phoenix Force lion was making his way down the ramp to the loading bay when he saw someone moving toward him out of the corner of his eye. Instinctively McCarter ducked, dropping to a crouch and rolling to his left as an ominous dark shape passed overhead. The shape landed on its feet and turned to attack at the same time the Briton came out of his roll.

Something whooshed through the air and McCarter felt his shirt and jacket tear at the sleeve near his shoulder. A stinging pain burned over his flesh along the path of the tear. The shape was almost upon him as McCarter aimed his Ingram and worked the trigger.

Three rounds of pure devastation met the shape head-on. A startled voice groaned in what sounded like Japanese and the shape merged with the inclined floor of the ramp.

McCarter sensed another presence rushing to attack him. He turned, swiveling to stop his unseen foe, the M-10 in his hands feeding the darkness a 9mm helping of parabellum lightning.

Again McCarter's swift reflexes saved his life. A loud shout of pain erupted less than five feet away. Dead-weight smacked concrete and something metallic clattered across the floor to McCarter.

The Englishman's eyes flicked downward to the faint outline of the object at his feet. His toes curled in his shoes as he recognized what it was…a *katana*, long sword of the legendary samurai.

A barrage of gunfire came from the entrance to the warehouse. More shots answered immediately in return. A cry of agony echoed in response.

"Liu-shen!" hollered a distant voice, this time in Chinese.

McCarter frowned, ignoring the flesh wound on his left shoulder. Had he actually heard one of their foes yell out a warning in *Chinese*? Yes, he was certian of it. And earlier, the first assailant he met had cried out in Japanese after being hit.

Then there was the *katana* to consider. For some un known reason Chinese and Japanese forces were working together. For some unknown reason... And then the truth rushed over McCarter like an ice-water shower.

"Bloody hell!" the Briton exclaimed. "TRIO!"

If he held any doubts as to the true identity of the enemy Phoenix Force faced, these fell to the wayside as the whirring of powerful generators suddenly came on and a great bank of lights along the ceiling began flooding the warehouse.

McCarter blinked, his eyes adjusting to the unexpected brightness. Thirty feet away, next to a well-cured hand of tobacco, a black-suited Mongolian was in the process of blasting him into the afterlife with a Type 56 assault rifle.

Like he had springs mounted on his heels, McCarter turned and jumped, clearing the border of the loading bay and running for cover as the Mongolian opened fire. Bullets from the Communist Chinese copy of the Soviet AK-47 appeared to follow the anxious Londoner every step of the way.

McCarter dived behind a tall shipping crate and hugged the floor as slugs from the Type 56 repeatedly gouged holes from the source of his protection. A storm of splinters rained upon his back as the crate was torn apart.

The overzealous Mongol was so intent on killing his enemy that he failed to conserve any ammunition for an emergency; something he experienced to the highest degree when his assault rifle's magazine coughed dry and an angry McCarter rejoined the fight.

Twitching like a broken marionette, the Mongolian caught a fistful of Ingram heartstoppers. The Type 56 raced its owner to the warehouse floor and lost.

Gary Manning pulled away from the controls to the overhead lighting in time to see the Mongolian wielding the Type 56 bite the dust. Like McCarter, the Canadian had drawn his own conclusions regarding the identity of their enemy.

The swarm of killers inside the warehouse had to be members of TRIO. Accept that, and so many other pieces to the puzzle of their mission fell into place.

Phoenix Force had originally clashed with the trinity of Oriental gangsters in San Francisco. That TRIO would be in the Philippines *and* responsible for the assault against the *Bruja del Mar* made every kind of sense. TRIO had resorted to piracy in the past, and establishing a base of operations in the Philippines would amount to setting up shop in the criminal cartel's own backyard.

"Kiayi!"

A TRIO troublemaker emerged from behind a row of stacked boxes and attacked, lunging for Manning's chest with a deadly samurai knife. Manning handily sidestepped the thrusting blade at the last possible moment, moving to the side and pushing against the killer's knife arm, while simultaneously popping off a point-blank shot with the Eagle.

The .357 slug burrowed through the assassin's right cheek and crashed out the upper left side of his skull. Bone fragments did a confetti number in the air. An eye leaped from its socket. The fingers of the fist holding the knife snapped open, losing the blade. The killer died on his feet and corkscrewed to the floor.

"*Kiqyi yourself, chum*," Manning told the corpse.

Katz, Encizo and Calvin James were well inside the warehouse, searching for the NISA production room, when Manning got the lights on. The three Phoenix soldiers found themselves in the center of an aisle crammed with pallets of cigars packed for shipping. Many of the pallets were stacked on metal shelves rising more than forty feet above their heads.

They had battled a small segment of the enemy force upon first entering the warehouse, but had succeeded in avoiding detection since then. The lights coming on changed all that.

Two black-clad fighters, both Mongolian, charged down the pallet-lined aisle. One Mongol with murder on his mind was swinging a jagged-edged hatchet, while his partner posed a greater threat with a Communist Chinese Type 51 pistol.

The warehouse aisle behind the Stony Man superstars was equally dangerous as three scowling Chinese killers attacked from the rear. The nearest of the tabi-footed toughs sported a pair of ring knives worn over the middle finger of each hand. Although the double-edged blades were primarily designed for slashing, they could just as easily peel off a victim's skin, one bloody strip at a time.

The next Chinese thug carried a gleaming single-edged butterfly knife that resembled a short saber. Built to hack and slash an opponent to pieces, the butterfly knife featured a curved metal quillon, where the blade met the hilt, to protect the hand of its user.

The last of the killers infesting the warehouse aisle had another of the Type 56 assault rifles. The Chinese goon pushed the end of the rifle's safety selector lever to its center position, readying it for full autofire.

As they were assaulted from both sides at once the Phoenix Force triumvirate exploded into action. Katz's Uzi scored the initial knockdown, blazing into the belly of the Mongol with the Type 51 pistol. Four shots from the Israeli's subgun tried making a home there, but the Mongol would have gladly posted a No Vacancy sign after the first of the 9mm slugs began rearranging his internal organs.

A volcano of unbelievable pain captured the Mongol's universe as his kidneys, liver, gallbladder and spleen all traded places at once. The Type 51 discharged as he fell, drilling the gut-shot Mongol through the left foot. The Mongol did not mind. It was a relief for him to hurt somewhere else.

Calvin James and Rafael Encizo concentrated on eliminating the three Chinese at the rear. James's Colt Python delivered hell and thunder to the killer lashing out with the butterfly knife. James fired twice. Both .357 pile drivers entered his target's chest, bursting through the sternum and out each shoulder blade and reducing to gritty garbage all points in between. Killer and butterfly knife took their tumble together.

The Chinese with the assault rifle was Encizo's problem. The Type 56 was already beginning to fire when the Cuban's sound supressed MP-5 did the same thing. Bullets from the hastily aimed Kalashnikov-copy went high, missing Encizo's head by inches, the bore of the loosely held Type 56 climbing in spite of the relatively heavy weight of the gun. By the time the careless assassin finally had control of the gun, it was far too late to do him any good.

Encizo hosed the killer from the lower jawbone to right kneecap with a shower of lead from the MP-5. Struck in so many places at once, the Chinese died on his feet, but the momentum of his attack kept his body running forward long enough to collide with Encizo in a dead-weighted tackle.

Unable to prevent it, the Cuban went down, slamming against Katz as he hit the floor. His Heckler&Koch all but useless, Encizo fought to heave the unwanted burden of the dead Chinese from his chest. Encizo pushed and the body pinning him to the floor rolled free.

The Cuban rose to a sitting position just as the murderer with the ring knives kicked him to the floor again. Encizo felt his head crack on the concrete, and his vision blurred. He shook his head and had more than a rush of anxiety when he saw the Chinese fighter's ring knives spinning toward his face like the cutting blades on a pair of electric blenders.

Then James's Colt boomed against the side of the Chinese killer's head and the twin propellers of double-edged death stopped turning. Brains and bone chips splattered the pallets. The dead man's knees caved in and the body toppled onto one of the metal shelves.

Struck from behind by Encizo when the Cuban fell, Katz was momentarily thrown off balance—exactly the kind of opening the hatchet-swinging Mongol hit man was looking for. A vicious *yoko geri keage* side kick sent the Israeli's Uzi flying. Confidently assured of at least one kill, the Mongolian brought his hatchet over and down to behead the disabled "old" man.

Katz felt his Uzi torn from his grasp almost at the same instant the shadow of the descending hatchet crossed his face. Instinctively Katz raised his prosthetic arm in defense. Hatchet met steel in a bone-jarring collision as the blade of the Mongol's war weapon connected with the three-pronged hook on the end of Katzenelenbogen's artificial arm.

Katz grunted, the energy from having halted the hatchet's descent painfully vibrating all the way up to his right shoulder. The Israeli inhaled sharply and the Mongol pulled back on the hatchet to try again.

Katz charged beneath the uplifted arm holding the hatchet and stabbed out with his three-pronged hook. Pointed steel pierced the flesh of the Mongol's throat. Katz pushed farther. Blood spurted from the wound in a grim parody of a leaking faucet.

The Mongolian let go of the hatchet and grabbed for the Israeli's prosthesis. Katz flexed his right shoulder muscles and the three prongs digging into his enemy's throat closed and became one. The Mongol assassin gurgled. A spasm shook his body. His feet jerked uncontrollably. Katz withdrew his hooked prosthesis from what little remained of the dead man's throat and let gravity do the rest.

The senior Phoenix Force member recovered his Uzi, then turned to his companions.

"Muchas gracias, amigo," Encizo offered while James helped him to his feet.

"De nada," the black warrior said with a smile. "Katz?"

The Israeli nodded. "I'll live."

James indicated the body of the slain Mongolian. "He the dude with the hatchet?"

"Not anymore," Katz answered.

"Right," James agreed. "He got what he axed for."

Encizo stared at the lifeless body of the killer who had used the butterfly knives. The body's bare forearms were decorated with a series of bizarre tattoos, most of them serpentine in nature.

"You know who all these guys are with?" the Cuban questioned.

Katz softly replied, "I'm afraid so."

16

"Win some, lose some, mate."

McCarter watched the Mongol with the empty Type 56 stop too many bullets in too many places and die on the spot. The TRIO killer's body was racing for the cement floor when the Englishman made his move, vacating the dubious protection of the slug-riddled packing crate in favor of making his way farther into the warehouse.

At the opposite side of the building, not too far from where he had entered the Tabacadera Tobacco Company storehouse, McCarter heard what sounded like Manning's .357 firing once. This single blast seemed to trigger a wave of gunfire, coming this time from an area lined thick with pallets. The shooting spree lasted all of thirty seconds, then was over as suddenly as it had begun. McCarter turned from the fading noise of the gunfight and pressed on.

Keeping as near to the wall as possible, the Briton left the loading bay behind. Phoenix Force had seen more than a dozen TRIO assassins storm the warehouse. He could account for three enemy dead, and Manning's Eagle had probably claimed another. How many Phoenix Force foes had perished during the gunfight amid the pallets, McCarter could only guess. It was too much to expect, however, that all of the TRIO killers had been eliminated.

McCarter moved silently forward. It was strange, he thought, to be inside a building packed full of tobacco and not have the urge for a cigarette. He licked his dry lips and *did* wish for a drink of Coca-Cola.

A barrier of crates jutted out from the wall, blocking his progress. To continue on he would have to move around the crates. Somewhere ahead was the production room of the NISA secret police. McCarter was determined to find it.

His M-10 held at the ready, the Briton stepped away from the wall and began following the row of crates. Each of the crates was approximately seven feet high, stored one atop the other in piggyback fashion. Their placement in the warehouse created an L-shaped formation that prevented much of the overhead lighting from reaching the floor. As a result, McCarter found himself traveling along a shadowy path of semidarkness.

Wood creaked and the air above the Briton sang with menace. McCarter collapsed instantly to a prone position. The glint of something metallic flashed from the topmost crate. There was a noise that sounded like chain uncoiling, then the crunch of splintered wood just above McCarter's back.

The Englishman rolled upright. Embedded in the side of the crate next to him was an evil-looking short scythe. Attached to the sickle was a long silver chain. The lengths of the *kusarigama* climbed to the top of the crate riding piggyback where the chain's weighted end was wrapped in the clenched fist of a Chinese TRIO killer.

The Oriental assassin snarled and yanked on the chain, working the scythe free from where it was caught in the crate. McCarter's hands flew to the chain, then he braced his feet against the base of the sickle-busted crate and pulled down as hard as he could.

The length of chain snapped tight, twisting back and forth, its links digging into the flesh of McCarter's palms. The Briton redoubled his efforts, kicking out and away from the crate, bringing the full weight of his body to bear on the chain.

The Chinese at the opposite end of the *kusarigama* was drawn to the edge of the crate. Tabi-soled feet slid across the wood. The assassin bent at the waist, tipping forward. He lost his footing and was airborne.

McCarter tugged again on the chain, adding momentum to the TRIO tough. With arms windmilling to prevent the inevitable, the killer dropped more than seventeen feet to the unyielding concrete of the warehouse floor, landing on his head. Bones cracked upon impact. The body collapsed like a pile of dirty rags. Deep red liquid oozed from an ear.

McCarter released his hold on the chain in time to see another figure running at him from around the row of crates, the outline of a 9mm Nambu automatic clutched in his hand.

In a blinding blur of motion McCarter had the Ingram running a storm of interference between him and his Japanese opponent. The Nambu barked twice. One bullet tore at the fabric of the Englishman's jacket, while the follow-up shot from the Nambu struck the warehouse ceiling. After that it was all downhill for the dying Japanese criminal.

In a parting gesture of poetic justice, it was a 3-round burst from McCarter's Ingram that killed the TRIO assassin. Two 9mm parabellum missiles of death ventilated the target's lungs like a couple of freight trains roaring through rice paper. Ribs shattered as one of the bullets rushed out the back. The scapula deflected the second M-10 stinger and sent it tunneling in reverse to lodge in the left ventricle of the heart.

The third slug transformed the Nippon nasty's nasal cavity into one big ugly hole. The Nambu automatic clattered to the floor as its owner lost both the will and the ability to live.

"Heads up!" Manning's voice reached McCarter less than a heartbeat before the Canadian's .357 opened fire, booming twice in quick succession.

McCarter spun in a semicircle as another pair of TRIO's representatives from the Land of the Rising Sun tumbled to the floor from atop the crates. Both killers were goners before they hit the ground.

"Nice shot, Dead-eye," McCarter observed with a grin. "The others?"

"Haven't seen 'em," Manning replied. "What about the production room?"

"Still looking for it."

Together McCarter and Manning continued along the row of crates. When they came to the last of the wooden containers McCarter carefully made sure the way ahead was clear, then signaled for Manning to follow.

Directly before them was a low table sectioned off into twelve individual compartments, six to a side. Each compartment served as a work area where, during the day, dextrous Filipino women could roll tobacco leaf to produce the distinctively aromatic Philippine cigars.

As they approached the table, the Phoenix Force duo could see dozens of perfectly rolled panatelas lined up in each compartment. Silently McCarter scooped a handful of the cigars and put them into his pocket before moving on.

Beyond the rolling tables, another tall formation of packing crates blocked their way. More shots rang out to their right, from the portion of the warehouse reserved for the pallets, and then McCarter and Manning were around and past the wall of wooden crates and facing the entrance to the NISA production room.

The padded door to the government-sanctioned torture chamber was closed, but as they stepped forward the black-clad leg of a TRIO assassin suddenly kicked it open. The men of Phoenix Force tensed, prepared for an attack. Instead, a single Chinese member of TRIO's criminal network boldly walked from the production room to greet them.

McCarter and Manning watched as the lone Chinese came to a halt fifteen feet from where they were standing. In the assassin's hands was another of the sickle-chain weapons. It was impossible not to notice the blood dripping from the blade of the short scythe.

"Well?" an impatient McCarter finally said.

"Ah, you speak English," the Chinese replied.

"How 'bout that?" the Briton commented. "What shall we talk about?"

The TRIO assassin shifted his almond-colored eyes from McCarter to Manning. "My brothers?"

"All dead, mate. You're the last of the line. TRIO loses again."

A flicker of surprise registered on the killer's face. "You know of us, then."

"We met once," McCarter told him. "In San Francisco."

The chain rattled against the assassin's leg. "Your reputation precedes you. We did not know who to credit that victory to."

McCarter tightened his grip on his weapon. "You still don't, pal. Drop the chain. Don't make me kill you."

A thin smile formed on the criminal's face. "That decision," he stated, "is not yours."

Faster than either McCarter or Manning could move to stop him, the TRIO assassin moved, grasping the *kusarigama*'s scythe in both hands and lifting the cutting edge of the sickle to his neck. With his eyes blazing defiantly, he forced the blade into his throat and rapidly turned his head from left to right. The smile was still on his face as he settled into a sitting position and died.

Manning swallowed. "What a way to go."

"Chokes me up," McCarter noted.

They progressed past the body of the dead Chinese as Katz, Encizo and James emerged to join them. Rafael was massaging his hand against the back of his head.

"Gentlemen," Colonel Katzenelenbogen greeted the pair. "Pleased to see you."

"Call it a clean sweep for our side," Manning said. "Looks like our friend with the sore throat was the last of them."

"You guys know who they're with?" McCarter asked.

"TRIO," Calvin James returned as they all made their way to the production room. "We figured it out. What happened to your arm, David?"

McCarter stared down at the shoulder wound he had received. "A scratch."

"We'll see," James said.

The NISA production room was a certified disaster area. The bodies of three secret police, one of which was missing a right hand, were sprawled about the room in various poses of death. The New People's Army prisoner they had come to reclaim seemed an ideal candidate to follow in his tormentor's steps any second.

Still strapped to the metal bed frame, Eduard Ayala had sustained a mortal wound to the chest. Blood spurted from the wound with each gasping breath, running over his skin and raining in red drops to the floor. The Communist coughed and opened one eye **a** fraction of an inch.

"Me duele todo el cuerpo," Ayala groaned in pain. *"Necesito un médico."*

Encizo crossed to the dying man and spoke in Spanish, *"Me llamo Rafael."*

Ayala coughed again. *"Quiero ir al hospital."*

Encizo leaned nearer and told the man he could go to the hospital *after* he answered a question.

"¿Qué es eso?" The Communist's voice was fading fast.

Encizo quickly explained that he wanted to know where Ayala and his friends had acquired the gold.

The Communist slowly nodded and softly whispered the answer with his dying breath. Encizo brushed the dead man's eyelids closed, then rose to his feet.

"Well?" Calvin James asked the question on everyone's mind. "Did he tell you where the NPA got the gold from TRIO?"

"We go south," Encizo said. "To Davao City."

17

Sadatoshi Matsuno stared at the silent radio receiver and gritted his teeth in frustration. Something had gone wrong in Manila. There could be no other explanation. Matsuno had been waiting since midnight to learn that Major Cortega's captured NPA ally had been liquidated according to plan. Three long hours later, he was still waiting.

Matsuno flexed the fingers of both hands into angry fists. Somehow the eighteen TRIO assassins brought in from Hong Kong to handle the liquidation had failed. Eighteen of the toughest killers in the Orient had not been enough for the job. The mystery of their failure was more than Matsuno could stand.

Had the Filipino secret police proved so fierce that not a single TRIO assassin survived? No, Matsuno decided. By and large the men of Metrocom, NISA and ISAFP were a pack of incompetent bunglers. To think that *any* of their miserable ilk could defeat such a formidable TRIO force was to stretch the capabilities of the Filipino secret police into the realm of science fiction.

If the secret police were not responsible, then...*who was?* Sadatoshi shivered. Major Cortega had reported that his men in Manila had been attacked by a band of foreigners. Ten of Cortega's New People's Army soldiers had been slain in the battle. As to the identities of these interlopers, Cortega had no clues.

Had TRIO's envoys from Hong Kong encountered the same group of foreigners? It was possible, yes. And however unbelievable or humiliating the scenario might seem, if such a confrontation *had* taken place, it was also reasonable to assume that all of the TRIO assassins had been defeated.

Whoever these foreigners were, they represented a potentially hazardous unknown. Major Cortega's information regarding the outsiders had been nonspecific. All that bumbling idiot of a Communist could come up with was that the meddlers were not Filipino. Big deal. Matsuno could have produced more than that in his sleep.

Cortega did not know where the foreigners came from, why they had attacked the New People's Army in Manila, or even how many foreigners had participated in the assault. All in all, a disturbing lack of knowledge.

Sadatoshi regarded the silent radio receiver with a contemptuous frown. No news was bad news. If TRIO had not liquidated Cortega's captured ally as planned, then the threat still existed that a hostile force could be lead to TRIO's hideout in Mindanao. However slight that danger might be, Matsuno could not afford to overlook it. TRIO would have to vacate the hideout at once.

The Japanese glared a final time at the uncooperative radio receiver and stormed through the ruins of the Spanish fortress, alerting the rest of the men of his decision. One of the last to be notified was a sleeping Lieutenant Ferris.

"Prepare to depart," Sadatoshi informed the renegade ONI officer.

Ferris snapped awake and checked his watch. 3:00 A.M. The tone of Matsuno's voice betrayed the fact that all was not well.

Ferris stretched and rose to his feet. "Something happen?"

"I believe we are no longer safe from discovery here at the fortress," Matsuno replied. "Be prepared to leave in fifteen minutes."

"What's going on?" Ferris asked.

"There have been," Sadatoshi said, "incidents of grave concern in Manila. That is all you need to know. Fifteen minutes. You will be ready."

Ferris nodded.

Matsuno turned and made his way back to the radio room. His superiors, Shimo Goro, Wang tse Tu and Tosha Khan, would have to contacted. While Matsuno sincerely regretted having to inform his bosses of what had obviously transpired in Manila, he felt assured the TRIO overlords would agree with his decision to vacate their fortress hideaway. At any and all costs the treasure from the *Bruja del Mar* must not be lost. Sadatoshi knew that as well as anyone.

As Matsuno passed one of the many TRIO fighters under his command inspiration struck. He turned back and spoke to the man.

"Find Major Cortega," Sadatoshi instructed. "Bring him to me. I will be at the radio."

As the TRIO fighter hurried to do Matsuno's bidding, the Japanese *yakuza* commander smiled. If that pighead Cortega could not be obliged to provide TRIO with something as elementary as reliable information, then perhaps the good comrade could accommodate TRIO in another way.

"I CAN'T ASK YOU to come with us, Mahmud," Mc-Carter said. "You've helped us more than enough already."

"Some help," the Briton's Bajau friend protested. "I shuttle you around town, fire a shotgun a couple of times and get you set up here at the Bomba. You would have done as much for me; you *have* done much more. I don't see how you can refuse my offer, David. If you and your friends must go to Davao City, then it would be prudent on your part to take me with you."

"I don't want to see you killed, Mahmud," McCarter said.

Mahmud chuckled. "We agree on that, at least. I have no desire to see you killed, either. And if there is the slightest chance that my going along with you and your friends could prevent such a tragedy, then I must listen to my heart and obey the message."

The Englishman threw his hands into the air. "What kind of bloody logic is that, Mahmud? The truth is we don't know what to expect once we reach the south. The bunch we're hoping to find down there is as vicious a mob of killers as we've ever come up against. Anything could happen."

"Precisely why I should be with you," Mahmud insisted. "You are in the Philippines, David. My homeland. I understand aspects of my country you could never hope to. Also, not every Filipino speaks English or Spanish. If you need a translator in a hurry, not only might you have trouble locating one, but you would have no guarantee they could be trusted once they were found. With me along for the ride, I am close by and my loyalty is above reproach."

Mahmud looked McCarter straight in the eyes. "When I needed your help in Hong Kong, you did not hesitate to give it. I do not hesitate to offer my help to you now. That our paths have crossed again is no accident. There is reason for everything. I believe we have met again so that I would have the opportunity to repay your past generosity. All I ask is to be given the chance to do that."

"All right, all right," McCarter said. "Let's say I agree to let your accompany us to Davao City. Will you prom ise not to stick your neck out and take any damn fool chances?"

Mahmud laughed and placed a hand on his friend's shoulder.

"Surely," he began, "you know me better than to ask such a question, David."

"That's what I was afraid you'd say," McCarter muttered.

18

Major Carlos Cortega, waiting with his men at a Davao City intersection, could not get over how lucky he was. In the middle of the night he had been roused from his sleep and firmly requested to put in an appearance before Sadatoshi Matsuno at the ruins of the Spanish fortress.

Normally Cortega would have objected. TRIO calling unannounced at such a late hour reflected a complete lack of respect for one of his stature, but Cortega had kept quiet. He had not achieved his rank in the New People's Army by stupidly passing up opportunity whenever it dropped on his doorstep.

Cortega arrived and was speaking with Matsuno by three twenty-five that morning. The first thing the NPA officer noted upon entering the ruins was that it seemed as though everyone at the TRIO camp was awake. Opportunity was knocking, all right, and Cortega was determined to be the first to open the door.

"Good morning," Matsuno greeted him. "I trust I didn't disturb too much of your sleep?"

"I was told it was urgent we talk," Cortega said. They were in a small chamber he knew had been used as a radio room, yet now the room was bare. "Naturally, once I learned you had need of my counsel, a full night's sleep was unimportant."

"Spoken like a true friend, Major Cortega."

"As well as a businessman," Cortega acknowledged. "What does my visit here this morning have to do with the New People's Army?"

"I have had some unfortunate news regarding your associate being held captive by the Filipino secret police."

"TRIO's attempts to liquidate him failed?"

"TRIO never got the chance to perform the deed, I'm afraid."

"Most strange," Cortega admitted, "especially since you assured me it was a problem TRIO would easily solve."

"And we would have," Matsuno continued, "but when my men reached the tobacco warehouse your comrade was nowhere to be found."

"That's impossible! My sources could not have been mistaken. Eduardo Ayala was scheduled for a NISA production room session last night at the Tabacadera Tobacco Company warehouse—"

"You didn't let me finish." Matsuno cut Cortega off. "I did not say this Ayala fellow of yours had not been at the warehouse, I only said he was not there when my men arrived. By then, all of the Filipino secret police on the scene were dead or dying and Ayala was gone."

"What do you mean 'gone'?"

"The only surviving NISA agent TRIO discovered reported the warehouse had been attacked by a foreign combat force," Matsuno elaborated. "In the ensuing fight the secret police were defeated by this band of foreigners and Ayala was abducted. We can only speculate what became of your comrade after that. The NISA agent died before he could reveal more."

"It does not sound good," Cortega concluded. "With Ayala still alive the path back to this fortress remains

open. And what about these 'foreigners' you mentioned? Surely they must be the very same troublemak-
ers who assaulted the NPA at the Intercontinental Hotel
Tuesday night!''

"My feelings exactly," Matsuno confessed. "Which is
why I sent for you. If the foreigners have extracted certain damaging information from this Ayala, then we have
to assume that they will strike here next."

"Which explains the reason for all the activity at this
time of the morning. TRIO is pulling out."

"Before the neighborhood becomes too crowded," the
Japanese *yakuza* was quick to add. "TRIO cannot
properly conduct its business with the threat of a potential attack always over its head. We shall retire to a less
accessible location."

"Of course," Cortega said. "TRIO is leaving before
the weather becomes too warm. Hmmm?"

"As you say, Major. And that is the true reason I have
asked to speak to you now. I would like to propose another business arrangement between TRIO and the New
People's Army."

"Oh?"

"Yes. Since it is highly probable the foreigners responsible for our mutual concern will eventually make
their way to Mindanao, I would like to hire you and the
NPA to prepare a suitable welcome for them. Because
they have already cost the New People's Army close to a
dozen lives, I am sure you would want to return the favor anyway. It is a question of honor. But to make your
participation in this matter even more assured, I am
willing to offer you additional piecees of TRIO's
treasure.''

"Why should TRIO be willing to pay the NPA to deal with the foreigners?" Cortega asked. "If you and your men are no longer here, what difference does it make?"

"These foreign meddlers, whoever they are," Matsuno answered, "are most persistent. If they are not stopped when they reach Mindanao, there is the possibility they will seek out TRIO's new headquarters at a later date. I would just as soon deal with the problem now, rather than in the future. However, if you think the New People's Army would prefer not to involve itself further in TRIO's affairs, then I understand completely."

"Not so fast," Cortega interrupted. "How many additional pieces of TRIO's treasure were you suggesting be turned over to the NPA?"

"We already gave you five of the gold objects."

"All of which were lost in Manila."

"Yes, well there is nothing I can do about that. What would you say to having the five gold objects you lost replaced with another five of equal value?"

Cortega shook his head. "I would say the New People's Army could do better. TRIO started with twenty precious articles of gold. You should still have fifteen left."

"As we do, Major, but certainly you can't expect our entire treasure as payment for something the NPA should reasonably want to do free. You did, after all, lose nearly twelve men to these foreigners."

"And run the risk of losing even more if we clash with them again," Cortega countered. "But now it is you who jump to conclusions. I wouldn't dream of accepting TRIO's entire treasure as payment for confronting the foreigners."

"That is most…"

"But I wouldn't hesitate to take close to half. TRIO has fifteen golden treasures of art; the New People's Army will accept seven of them to do as you wish. Pay us this amount and you can rest easy that, once TRIO has departed, I and my NPA followers will prepare a suitable welcome for these foreigners, should they arrive in Mindanao. Considering that the danger will be all ours, I think the fee exceedingly fair. Don't you agree?"

And of course, Sadatoshi Matsuno had agreed to Cortega's terms. What other choice did TRIO have? So, Cortega was paid. And soon after that Matsuno and the rest of TRIO departed from the ruins of the fortress and disappeared down the mountains into Davao City.

Where TRIO had journeyed from there, Cortega did not know. All that mattered to him was that he had succeeded in skimming off two of the seven gold art objects from TRIO for his own personal nest egg. Once again, the future seemed bright. After he and his men had disposed of the foreigners, his esteem within the NPA would rise an important notch higher.

The New People's Army was, as yet, without a single unifying leader that the Filipino populace could rally behind. To Major Carlos Cortega's way of thinking, this was a deplorable condition begging for change, but it did not represent an insurmountable problem.

When the time came for someone to lead the New People's Army to victory in the Philippines, Cortega knew just the right man for the job.

19

Mahmud hit the brakes the instant he saw the two trucks pull across the intersection.

"Hold on to your hats, gentlemen!" the able Bajau called. "We've got trouble!"

Mahmud cut the wheel hard to the right, hopping the curb and skidding to a halt after plowing through a sari-sari stand selling soft drinks and sewing supplies. The proprietor of the demolished roadside stall grabbed his money till and ran.

"I love surprises!" McCarter remarked, watching the wooden sides of each truck bed suddenly sprout a crop of armed commandos.

The four doors of Phoenix Force's rented Chevrolet popped open simultaneously. McCarter and Calvin James, who had been riding up front, darted for the tempting entrance of a butcher shop. Gary Manning and Rafael Encizo sought refuge behind the counter of an outdoor restaurant. One look at the weapons the Canadian and the Cuban wielded sent the terrified patrons of the eatery fleeing with fright.

Yakov Katzenelenbogen and Mahmud leaped from the opposite side of the Chevy as the gunmen from the trucks began firing. Cars traveling along the street rear-ended one another and were hastily abandoned as drivers ran for safety. One hapless man was slain by a shot through the brain as he rushed from his car.

Bullets from enemy assault rifles and submachine guns stabbed into metal and upholstery as Katz and Mahmud made their way across the street. McCarter unleashed a lead escort for the Israeli and his Bajau friend with his Ingram, while Encizo did the same with his Heckler&Koch MP-5. Manning was using his Eagle .357, and James was looking for blood with the compact "little brother" of the M-10, the Ingram M-11 machine pistol.

"Nice to feel wanted, isn't it?" James said, catching one of the attackers on the nearest truck with a triple-burst of destruction from the M-11. The target tossed his rifle aside and slapped his hands to the geyser spurting from his throat, then flipped from the back of the truck onto the pavement.

McCarter and James pulled farther into the doorway as enemy bullets gouged a strip of jagged holes in the edge of the building. More bullets blew apart the shop's front window. Glass shattered and chunks of raw beef and pork were knocked swinging on their hooks.

Katz and Mahmud ducked behind the crunched-in trunk of an abandoned car. The Phoenix Force unit commander's Uzi was clutched in his left hand. Mahmud's sawed-off shotgun was tucked under his arm.

The gas tank of the car at the head of the line ignited and exploded with a whoosh of bright orange flame and thick black smoke. Twisted metal and bits of windshield rained from the sky.

Katz motioned to Mahmud. "Let's go!"

With the shock waves from the exploding gas tank ringing in their ears, the two men made their move, running as fast as they could for the protection to be found on the other side of the street. Bullets chased their progress like hungry shadows. One slug sheared a button from the Israeli's coat. Another clipped the heel of Mahmud's right shoe. They reached the doorway of a barbershop and dived through a second ahead of lead hailstorm.

Katz rolled to his knees and climbed to his feet. "Still glad you came with us, Mahmud?"

The Bajau grinned as he stood. "What do you think?"

The driver of the truck closest to the barbershop saw Katz and Mahmud disappear inside. The Communist grunted to himself with satisfaction. A narrow alley ran behind the row of stores on his side of the street. If he could reach the alley it would be easy to sneak into the barbershop from the rear.

Encizo spotted the driver of the truck on his left make a break for the alley and swore out loud when his H&K failed to bring the driver down. *"¡Leche!"*

Manning dropped behind the counter to reload. "What's up?"

Encizo knelt beside Manning. "One of the bastards hightailed it around the corner. My money says he's gonna trying sneaking up on Katz and Mahmud through the rear of the barbershop."

The Canadian shook his head. "Too damn much firing to shout across the street. Katz would never hear us."

A stray bullet zinged off a faucet and ruptured the pipe it was attached to. Cold water squirted into the air. An iron skillet hanging on a wall was hit dead center and fell with a crash to the floor.

"So, what do we do about warning Katz?" Encizo wondered.

The Canadian finished reloading his Magnum. "At this point...nothing."

JONATHAN PATRAS gripped his AK-47 tighter and swiftly made his way along the alley leading to the rear of the barbershop. It had been close. One of the foreign dogs had nearly chopped him down when he made his move, but now he was home free. Soon, two of the devils the NPA had been hired to kill would be dead.

Patras slowed as he reached the screen door at the back of the barber's. He pressed himself against the building and lightly tested the door with his fingertips. It pushed in slightly, then bounced out again, telling Patras the door was unlocked.

He stood beside the door and listened. Submachine-gun fire erupted inside. Good. That meant the enemy was distracted, paying too much attention to the front of the building, ignoring the potential dangers at their back. It was a situation Patras aimed to take advantage of.

Sucking air into his lungs to steel himself for what he was about to do, Patras held his assault rifle in one hand and slowly opened the door with the other. He tensed, waiting to see if anyone had noticed. No one had. The New People's Army Communist smiled. This was going to be easy.

Patras took another deep breath and eased his head around the edge of the door and into the barbershop—an action that brought his face less than two inches from the double barrels of a sawed-off shotgun. Patras gulped and lost control of his bowels.

"Goodbye!" Mahmud whispered, then triggered both barrels of the shotgun in quick succession.

The results of the twin blasts were immediate, decapitating the Communist where he stood and flinging his headless corpse in a sloppy fall to the pavement in the alley. Mahmud replaced the gun's spent shells, scooped up the dead man's Kalashnikov, then hurried back to the front of the barbershop.

"Did you get him?" Katz asked.

Mahmud nodded. "It was a sheer delight!"

ANOTHER FUSILLADE OF ENEMY BULLETS plowed into the body of Phoenix Force's Chevy. Glass burst and shattered as the rear window was blown away. The left front tire exploded with a boom. The car's radiator was punctured a half dozen times and started to leak.

"I'm glad *I* didn't sign for it," Calvin James noted.

"No sweat off my nose," McCarter returned. "I may have signed for the car hire all right, but I signed your name!"

James laughed, "Yeah, sure."

McCarter emptied the M-10 magazine at the enemy trucks, then pulled back as more unfriendly bullets peppered the interior of the butcher shop. As the tough Briton changed sticks on the Ingram, he spoke to Calvin "It's no good."

"What's that?"

"I just stitched the wooden sides of the beds of both lorries with enough lead to sink a battleship. But zip. Nothing happened. Far as I can tell none of the men using 'em for cover have been hit. The only ones any of us have been able to plug have been the careless ones who have shown their faces."

"The backs of the trucks could be armor plated on the inside," the black Phoenix warrior suggested.

"That's what I thought. In which case we'll run out of ammo before we get all the bastards."

"You think the trucks are plated underneath?"

McCarter's eyes lit up. "Let's find out."

MAJOR CARLOS CORTEGA mentally counted his dead and resisted the urge to chew his fingernails. Some leadership image that would present. Damn Matsuno's miserable hide! Already Cortega had lost five of his men. And since the one-armed older man was still alive and kicking with his submachine gun in the entrance to the barbershop, that probably indicated that Jonathan Patras was gone, too. Six of his men dead. Half of his strike team slaughtered. It was unthinkable!

Nobody could convince Cortega that Matsuno had told him everything he knew about the foreigners. That damned Japanese crook! No wonder Matsuno and TRIO had left the ruins of the Spanish fortress in such a hurry. These deadly foreigners represented more than just a handful of men with guns; they fought with the fury of an entire army.

Normally Cortega would have used three or four times as many men for an ambush. He cursed his impatience. If he had let the foreigners come to him at the fortress in the mountains, he would have had upward of fifty men or more at his command. Bringing that many NPA regulars into Davao City for the hit, though, was impossible.

The Philippine government's troops were a clumsy lot as a rule. Still, their numbers were sufficiently large in this part of Mindanao to dictate caution. Not every Filipino was ready to embrace the ideals of the New People's Army, and until that day came to pass Cortega, and those like him, would have to be wary in order to survive.

A stream of bullets rang against the metal plating protecting the truck bed. No one fighting from the rear of the truck was injured. The NPA soldier next to Cortega began to rise so he could fire back, but quickly changed his mind when more enemy bullets creased the rim of the truck bed.

"What do we do now, Major?" the anxious Communist asked.

Not knowing what to answer, Cortega scooted away. A narrow gap between where the bed met with the truck's cab provided a relatively safe view of the ambush site. His eye watered as black smoke from the wreckage of the burning automobile blew his way. Cortega licked his lips and swallowed, tasting gasoline.

The smoke cleared and he could see the front of the butcher shop. Cortega blanched as two arms appeared in the doorway and hurled a pair of metal objects at his truck. Instantly, Cortega realized he had the answer to his soldier's question

"We die," Cortega said. "We..."

Then the two M-26 fragmentation grenades McCarter and James had thrown at the truck detonated, their explosions coming so close together as to be indistinguishable from each other. Shards of shrapnel pierced the underbody of the truck, ripping into the vehicle's fuel tank with the roar of a thundercrack. Sparks danced to the tune of the blast and the fuel tank ignited.

With all the power of a miniature volcano the truck blew up, taking Major Carlos Cortega's career in the New People's Army to new and unwanted heights. Cortega was launched into the sky like a rag doll shot from a cannon, parts of his writhing body dismembering in the air before his mutilated torso completed its brief flight and plummeted like a sack of wet dirt to the ground.

The Communist soldier next to Cortega died doing a perfect imitation of a human fireball, while the stunned NPA veteran next to him was more or less vaporized on the spot. The three Reds using the second truck for cover fared no better. Two of the New People's Army diehards did exactly that when scraps of flaming debris from the grenade-blown truck settled over their soon-to-be-fried bodies in a hot embrace of death.

The last Communist perished as he tried escaping the sudden destruction and climbed straight into the path of a 3-round burst from Katzenelenbogen's Uzi. His body slumped over the slats bordering the truck bed and began to cook.

McCarter slapped James on the back. "That's the lot of 'em, sport. Time to go."

Together the Briton and the American exited the shambled interior of the bullet-damaged butcher shop and joined the remaining members of the Phoenix Force on the street outside. To a man the team had emerged from the ambush unscathed. Even Mahmud, much to McCarter's relief, had pulled through the attack without a scratch.

"She's a dead loss." Manning kicked the single remaining intact tire of their rented Chevrolet.

"We'll borrow one of the others, then," Mahmud said, tossing the keys of the Chevy to McCarter. The Bajau then ran to the end of the row of abandoned cars and called out, "Down here! The key's in the ignition. Come. We must hurry!"

McCarter unlocked the Chevy's trunk and everyone removed their gear. Wind blew acrid smoke from the burning trucks in their faces. Sirens could be heard in the distance. Genuine thunder rumbled overhead.

Their equipment in tow, the Phoenix Force vets hustled down the street. Mahmud had turned their getaway car around and was frantically waving his arm out the window, urging them to greater speed. A warm drizzle of rain began to fall.

"I meant to ask," Encizo said to Katz as they ran, "about that guy that tried for the barbershop through the alley. What happened?"

The Stony Man pros reached the getaway car and piled in, Mahmud screeching away from the site of the ambush with a squeal of burning rubber.

"So, what about the guy in the alley?" Encizo asked again.

"It was a close shave," Katz reported, "but Mahmud took care of him."

Mahmud laughed. "Now, aren't you glad I came along?"

None of Phoenix Force could argue about that.

20

David McCarter could tell from Mahmud's expression that all was not well.

"Let's hear it," the Briton said as Mahmud returned to the LABAN safehouse. "I recognize that 'good news–bad news' look when I see it. What's up?"

Mahmud crossed to a rattan chair and sat down. "We got here too late. The men belonging to TRIO had already departed from Davao City before we arrived."

"Swell," Calvin James said and whistled. "I hope to hell that ain't the good news."

"TRIO chartered a private yacht at seven o'clock this morning. They were on the sea by eight."

"How many in the party?" Katz questioned.

"Roughly fifteen men," Mahmud said. "All equally divided in nationality between Chinese, Japanese and Mongolian."

Manning sighed. "That's TRIO, all right. And I imagine they carried on board a certain amount of unspecified cargo?"

"They did for a fact," the Bajau confirmed. "No one can say for sure what cargo the passengers were carrying, though, because all of it was crated."

"Splendid," Rafael Encizo commented. "Obviously TRIO got antsy after our showdown with their boys at the tobacco warehouse. When TRIO-south failed to hear from TRIO-north, they pulled up stakes and hightailed it off Mindanao.''

"What about the ambush at the intersection?" asked Manning. "They weren't TRIO."

"They were more of your friends from the New People's Army. The whole of Davao City is talking about it. One of the Communists killed was a major named Cortega. Somewhat of a big shot. He had a handsome bounty on his head. It is said the government troops are more than eager to turn over the reward to us."

"I'll bet they are," McCarter muttered, then turned to Mahmud. "What about the good news, then?"

"Yes, of course." The Bajau beamed. "Although the men you seek have made a swift departure, that does not mean they have vanished altogether. I mentioned how they chartered a private yacht, and this is true. What is also true is that prior to setting off in the Davao Gulf the owner of the yacht was required by the Filipino Port Authority to list the vessel's destination."

"That's terrific, Mahmud," McCarter congratulated his friend. "Where's the yacht going?"

"Borneo," Mahmud replied.

"Can you be a little more specific?" Katz requested.

"No need to. I have the situation well in hand. TRIO, you see, sails for where my people live. Once they reach the islands of the Sulu Archipelago, then TRIO is in the Bajaus' neighborhood. TRIO cannot travel there for any extended length of time without my people knowing about it."

"TRIO has too much of a jump on us to catch them by sea," James decided. "Are there any airports out that way we could fly to?"

"The best would be the one in Bato Bato."

"Where's that?" Encizo asked.

Mahmud answered, "On the island of Tawitawi."

SADATOSHI MATSUNO stood on the bridge of the *El Astro* and reread the message transmitted from Davao City. He wadded the communique into a crumpled ball of paper and threw it away.

Major Carlos Cortega was dead, killed along with approximately a dozen of his men during an abortive ambush against the group of foreigners Matsuno had been expecting. While the identities of the foreigners continued to be an enigma, their actual numbers did not. Eyewitness accounts revealed that Cortega and his men had died trying to eliminate five non-Filipinos and one native. Six men? Were there no more? Apparently not.

Color rose to Matsuno's face as it flushed with a combination of embarrassment and anger. If he were to believe his source of information in Davao City, responsibility for the deaths of eighteen of his men in Manila, as well as all of the slain NPA, could be laid at the feet of these five foreigners.

In light of this revelation Matsuno was almost ashamed to admit that he had ordered the dismantling of TRIO's base in Mindanao. In his eagerness to protect the treasure from the *Bruja del Mar*, had he overreacted? Not really, if he could judge as accurate the report from Davao City.

Who were these five who fought unafraid against TRIO and the New People's Army? Where did they come from? Where had they first learned of the disappearance of the *Bruja del Mar*'s precious cargo?

A distinct feeling of uneasiness settled over Matsuno's shoulders. Whoever these five foreigners were, they had miraculously defied *every* obstacle put in their path to stop them. And now Major Cortega was dead.

While Sadatoshi did not mourn Cortega's passing, he did feel a belated sense of compassion for the late NPA commander. Cortega had been hopelessly outclassed by his opponents and, as far as Matsuno could tell, would have bungled the ambush with two or three times as many men at his side. Not even the help of, say, eighteen TRIO warriors would have made a difference.

So, Cortega was dead and the foreigners who killed him were very much alive. What would the foreign devils do now? TRIO's trail had ended in Davao City. What were the foreigners to do? Search the whole of the Pacific?

Sadatoshi Matsuno frowned and was grateful not to be in Mindanao.

21

The plan Gary Manning came up with called for a couple of high-powered catamarans, the kind favored by the area's smugglers and pirates. The difficulty with the Canadian's scheme was that smugglers and pirates were notoriously unenthusiastic about lending out their boats.

"It's not exactly like we can pop on down to *Smugglers Rents*," McCarter had pointed out.

"No problem," Manning assured his British friend. "If we need a couple of catamarans, we can always hijack them."

Which was what Phoenix Force was preparing to do now—beat the pirates and smugglers at their own game. Hidden within the sheltered enclosure of Mahmud's *lipa*, a typical Bajau fishing vessel, Manning and the others were patiently biding their time, waiting for the opportunity to lure one of the contraband-carrying catamarans in their direction.

Prior to flying from Davao City to the small airport on Tawitawi, Katz had placed an international telephone call to his "Uncle Hal" in the United States. The information relayed during the carefully coded five-minute conversation proved enlightening. After Katz related what Phoenix Force knew of TRIO's involvement with the disappearance of the *Bruja del Mar*, Brognola brought the Israeli up-to-date on developments at his end of the line.

For starters, the air-and-sea search for the missing Colombian ship had been called off. Colombia had lodged an official letter of complaint with the U.S. government protesting the incident, and was asking that the United States assume full responsibility for the loss of the *Bruja del Mar*'s crew and treasure. In addition, the Brandywine Initiative, which would establish new guidelines for Colombia's internal crackdown on the manufacture and trafficking of illegal drugs, showed every indication of falling apart on the bargaining table if the *Bruja del Mar*'s precious cargo was not recovered.

Continued investigation of the two ONI men, Ferris and Mitchell, had determined that both officers visited Tokyo at least twice during the past six months; their last journey to Japan was made just one week prior to the ONI lieutenants' assignment aboard the *Bruja del Mar*. Knowing TRIO had masterminded the plot against Colombia's floating museum provided a probable explanation behind the Tokyo trips made by the ONI officers.

Hal Brognola's final piece of news was of most concern to Phoenix Force. The treasure taken from the *Bruja del Mar* was going to be auctioned. Interested underground art dealers were to meet in Hong Kong on the following Saturday where they would then be transported, supposedly by air, to the auction's location. While previous reports hinted that the auction would not happen for another couple of weeks, Brognola speculated that its rescheduling was prompted by pressure being applied by Phoenix Force.

"You're getting close," Brognola had said.

"Closer than they know," Katz agreed.

And so Phoenix Force was in Mahmud's *lipa*, drifting with the current in the middle of the night, waiting for the chance to put the first stage of Manning's plan into action.

While Mahmud had eagerly accompanied the Stony Man team through a number of dangerous confrontations since their arrival in the Philippines, the true test of the Bajau's courage came when it was time for him to put his twenty-five-foot boat out to sea. Enjoying the stomach-churning rise and fall of the waves as much as Katz liked flying, Mahmud settled down and forgot about losing his supper overboard only after Calvin James had provided an antinausea capsule from his medical kit.

"Cuts the motion from the ocean," James advised upon their departure. And the capsule had done the trick. At sea for the better part of three hours, Mahmud had exhibited no signs of illness.

"Oh for the life of a sailor," McCarter softly sang as another wave rocked the vessel and Mahmud poked his head into the boat's tiny enclosure.

"They come," was all the Bajau said, and then he was back outside doing whatever Bajau fishermen did in the middle of the night.

At first, even with their trained sense of hearing, the men of Phoenix Force heard nothing, but about a minute later the quiet chugging sounds of twin Mercedes-Benz engines greeted their ears. Mahmud waited until the smuggler's craft was within a hundred yards of the *lipa*, then picked up a ladle and twice banged it loudly against the side of a hollow pipe attached to his boat.

Seconds after Mahmud hit the pipe, the chugging engines of the smuggler's catamaran slowed and changed direction, turning toward the *lipa*. Playing the role of frightened fisherman to the hilt, Mahmud huddled in fear at the far end of his boat as the smugglers approached. The catamaran's engines cut to an idle and a surly male voice called across the water.

"Ho, fisherman!" the voice challenged. "And what brings you out in such miserable weather?"

"Forgive me, sir," Mahmud answered, "but I am merely trying to catch enough fish for my family and I to live on."

"Ha!" the arrogant smuggler laughed. "Not much of a fisherman! Where is your catch?"

"Sadly, the spirits of the sea have not smiled on me this voyage. I have been out for a total of four days now and nothing. As you can see, my drying racks are bare."

McCarter nodded. Mahmud's "four days" was his friend's way of letting them know that there were four men aboard the catamaran.

"They *are* bare," the smuggler concurred, "but just the same, through your clumsiness at making a noise and letting us know you were here, you have interrupted our journey this evening. You have cost us precious travel time. I would never forgive myself if I simply turned our boat around and continued on our way without exacting some manner of payment from you. Do you understand?"

"Oh, I do, sir—" Mahmud's voice trembled as he swept his arms wide apart "—but as you can see, there is scant of value I can offer you."

"You try my patience, Bajau." The smuggler's tone grew angry.

Mahmud fell to his knees. "Ah, I beg you, kind sir. Do not shoot me. To do so would be a tragic waste of your bullets."

McCarter smiled grimly to himself. The smugglers were armed.

"Be quick and pay us for letting you live and we will be out of your life," the smuggler promised, then curiously asked, "What is it you keep within your shelter?"

Immediately Mahmud rose to his feet and stammered his reply. "Oh, believe me, sir, what I keep in my shelter is the last thing you would wish to find."

"Just as I thought," the smuggler boasted. "You *are* hiding something."

"No, sir," Mahmud protested. "I assure you I am not."

"I'll be the judge of that, Bajau. Stand aside. I'm coming aboard."

The catamaran engines revved slightly and Mahmud's boat tilted to the side as the smuggler hopped onto the *lipa*.

"Please, sir," Mahmud begged. "Leave me and my belongings alone. I am poor and my family..."

"Silence!" the smuggler ordered as he crossed to poke his head into the boat's small enclosure. "We shall see what we..."

The astonished smuggler gasped as Encizo grabbed the intruder's hair and held the sharp edge of a Gerber Mark I dagger to his throat. The Cuban hissed, warning the smuggler to be quiet.

"You speak English?" Encizo whispered. *"¿Habla usted español?"*

"Sí," the man croaked softly. *"Lo hablo."*

"Bueno." The Cuban smiled. "Then you understand when I tell you I'll cut your throat unless you do exactly as I say. Now, call to your friends. Tell them you need help hauling a heavy chest out on deck. Be very convincing, *señor*, or you will be very dead. *¿Comprende?"*

"*Sí,*" the smuggler assured him. "I do as you say."

The bottom-of-the-barrel pirate called out to his comrades and repeated Encizo's instructions to the letter. The Cuban yanked the smuggler inside the enclosure and took the knife from the man's throat. He suddenly swung his arm and rammed the butt of the Gerber into the goon's abdomen just above the groin. The smuggler doubled up with a groan and Encizo clipped him behind the ear and knocked the guy unconscious.

"This chest better not be just a bunch of old books and junk, Rico," one of the other smugglers announced as he crossed over to the *lipa* and shoved his head into the enclosure.

A black fist rocketed into the second smuggler's face. The stunned hoodlum staggered backward as Calvin James sprang forward and launched a tae kwon-do side kick to the creep's midsection. The smuggler wheezed breathlessly. James slammed a backfist to his opponent's jaw and kicked him again. The smuggler was propelled over the edge of the *lipa* and splashed through the surface of the water.

Encizo and David McCarter simultaneously burst from both sides of the enclosure. They aimed their machine pistols at the two remaining smugglers before the seagoing muggers could gather up their weapons. The smugglers raised empty hands in surrender.

"Jump, you bastards," McCarter ordered. "Jump overboard and start swimming for shore or we'll shoot your arse off that rig."

Encizo repeated the sermon in Spanish to be certain the smugglers understood what they had to do. The hoodlums hesitated, aware that there might be sharks in the water. However, they were certain of the gun-toting threat in front of them. The smugglers decided to take their chances with the fish and dived overboard.

"Everybody come on out and watch the final act of tonight's performance," McCarter called out.

Katz and Manning emerged from the enclosure to see the three smugglers swimming from view. James dragged the unconscious hoodlum into the open as McCarter slapped Mahmud on the back.

"Bloody good show, mate," the Briton told him. "Academy Award material."

"I guess it is the born actor in me." The Bajau shrugged and grinned.

"What'll we do with sleeping beauty here?" James inquired, referring to the unconscious smuggler.

"Wake him up so he doesn't drown when we throw him overboard," Manning explained. "And then we gotta get ready."

"Ready for what?" Mahmud asked.

"To do this all over again," the Canadian declared.

22

Moored in the clear warm waters a mile off the coast of Bunabunaan Island, south of Tawitawi, the motor yacht *El Astro* resembled a long silver specter upon the night sea. At seventy-five foot, powered by twin Detroit diesels, and featuring a full galley, three heads, two showers and five double staterooms, the custom-built yacht offered a wealth of luxury for TRIO's purposes.

At the moment, however, Sadatoshi Matsuno had little use for *El Astro*'s many comforts. It was after one in the morning. The auction to sell the golden art objects and jewels seized from the *Bruja del Mar* was not scheduled for another twelve hours. Three of his fourteen TRIO warriors on board were standing watch; the rest were asleep. Only Lieutenant Ferris and Matsuno occupied the bridge.

Matsuno sat, drumming his fingers rhythmically over the arm of his chair.

"You're making something out of nothing," Ferris said.

"Perhaps," Matsuno acknowledged. "Perhaps not. Each coin has two sides."

"And both sides can be lucky," Ferris countered, glancing out across the water to where the source of Matsuno's concern was anchored.

It was a catamaran, a twin-hulled powerboat of the kind preferred by smugglers. The craft had been there since eleven o'clock when it, and a boat very much like it, appeared from around the opposite side of Bunabu- naan Island.

Both of the high-powered catamarans cut their en- gines less than a mile from *El Astro*'s port side. Voices were heard. Two males. Each speaking what sounded from a distance like Spanish. The two men were moving back and forth from one boat to the other, but even with the aid of binoculars, the poor illumination afforded by the cloud-covered sky made it impossible to determine what the pair was up to.

After five minutes the first catamaran dropped an- chor. Then the two men boarded the second of the twin- hulled powerboats and were gone, speeding in a wide semicircle around TRIO's position before finally disap- pearing in the murky darkness altogether. The second catamaran had not been seen or heard from since.

El Astro's crew remained on alert for an hour before Sadatoshi called it off. Now only Matsuno and the three Mongolians standing watch paid any attention to the an- chored catamaran.

Ferris sat and studied Matsuno as the Japanese *yakuza* repeatedly drummed his fingers along the arm of his chair. Although Matsuno refused to admit it, TRIO was clearly on the run. Mighty TRIO, the outwardly invin- cible network of Oriental criminals Ferris had willingly betrayed his country for, was spending its days and nights chased by shadows.

How else could their sudden departure from Min- danao be explained? Or the way the auction of the *Bruja del Mar*'s treasure had been unexpectedly advanced by more than ten days? In Ferris's mind there could be no doubt. Matsuno and TRIO were running scared, behaving like fugitives. And if a danger existed that could cause TRIO to fear, then Ferris was smart enough to know that threat was real.

But from a smuggler's catamaran? Not likely. Counting himself, *El Astro* contained sixteen heavily armed men. For a single vessel of the catamaran's size, regardless of how many men she might conceal, to attack *El Astro* would be madness.

"Do you intend to watch the catamaran all night?" Ferris asked.

Matsuno nodded. "Curiosity demands I question why the catamaran has been left so near *El Astro*. The sea is sufficiently large for the smugglers to have anchored their boat virtually anywhere without intruding upon our space. Yet this is the course they have followed. I am not sure why they have done so, but I know there must be a reason. There always is. I do not believe in chance."

The Japanese suddenly jumped from his chair and pointed. "You see? It is just as I predicted!"

Even as Ferris and Matsuno stared at the nearby catamaran a great rumbling noise seemed to engulf them on *El Astro*'s bridge. A white wave of energy formed beneath the catamaran, lifting it into the air, pushing its entire length from the water.

The wave of brilliant energy turned scarlet under the boat, and then the sea about the smuggler's craft was rocked by multiple explosions, each blast more fearsome than the one before. They culminated in a rolling ball of orange flame that split the night in two, rising from the catamaran's fuel tanks and climbing into the sky.

Momentarily distracted by the spectacular destruction of the smuggler's craft, Matsuno thought to look over his shoulder.

"Nothing is an accident!" the Japanese shouted.

And off the starboard bow Ferris saw it too...the ominous black outline of the second catamaran, racing at top speed for *El Astro*!

23

The catamaran's Mercedes-Benz engines carried the boat skimming over the surface of the sea like an enormous flat stone. Mahmud was at the wheel, throttles running full, charging through the night for TRIO's yacht. The catamaran crested a wave, left the water, then slammed back down on course.

"Sorry for the bumpy ride!" Mahmud apologized above the noise of the nearby explosions.

"Just get us to the yacht!" McCarter hollered in response.

As Phoenix Force drew closer, Gary Manning opened fire with his H&K G-3. The Canadian's targets were the three men stationed on the *El Astro*'s foredeck. Typically, for nighttime sniping, Manning would have used a special Starlite infrared scope mounted on the G-3's barrel, but the incredible series of explosions taking place on the port side of the yacht made the Starlite unnecessary. Lined up against the flaming wreckage of the catamaran the TRIO warriors on the yacht's foredeck provided excellent targets.

Methodically working the H&K's two stage, creep-bang trigger, Manning emptied the rifle's 20-round magazine by going from one target to the next and back again. Given the uneven nature of the ride Mahmud was providing, many of the G-3's shots hit nothing.

In the end, though, Manning's talents as the Phoenix team's foremost sharpshooter won out, scoring the decisive hits the Canadian was looking for. One, two, and finally all three of his targets did the dance of death to the tune of repeated requests by the G-3's 150-grain bullets. Two toe-tapping TRIO silhouettes bopped till they dropped, while the third ended his dancing debut with a splash.

"My kind of music," Manning declared, reloading his Heckler& Koch.

The Canadian knew that the easy way to take out the TRIO savages on board *El Astro* was to frag the yacht with grenades from one end to the other, right down to the waterline. That would give TRIO's rats the fitting end they deserved, but at the cost of losing the *Bruja del Mar*'s priceless treasure.

So, it's business as usual, Manning thought as he finished reloading. *We do it the hard way.*

They were less than thirty yards from *El Astro*'s starboard ladder when two more of the TRIO toughs appeared, both of the Oriental criminal fanatics blazing away at the approaching catamaran with a pair of Shin Chuo Kogyo SMGs. Taking evasive action, Mahmud expertly cut the wheel hard to the right, then doubled back to the left, setting up *El Astro* for a broadside attack from McCarter's Ingram and Encizo's MP-5.

Trapping the Japanese subgunners in a blistering cross fire of lead, the Cuban and the Briton put any plans the pair of TRIO killers may have had for a future life on everlasting hold. The first murderer to bow out of the human race retired with a bloody third eye in the center of his forehead and nothing much to look at. His partner bought the farm and all the trimmings with a shot through the heart.

Both blights on humanity were getting into the swim of things as Mahmud brought the catamaran in for its final approach of the yacht, cutting in on the wheel and pulling back on the throttles, bringing the catamaran near enough for Phoenix Force to make use of *El Astro*'s starboard ladder.

David McCarter was the first to board the yacht, reaching the top of the ladder as a screaming Chinese killer ran at him from the stern.

"Aaaiiieee!" the TRIO assassin screamed as he attacked, unleashing a sickle-bladed *kusarigama* from the end of a chain.

The steel crescent struck McCarter's M-10, ripping the machine pistol from his grasp. The Briton did not give his attacker a chance to try again with the *kusarigama*. He did the unexpected and charged.

The TRIO warrior raised his chain-and-sickle weapon, but the Briton had already closed in. McCarter lashed a boot under the Oriental's rib cage. The killer groaned and slashed an iron ball at the opposite end of the chain. McCarter caught the hard metal sphere on a shoulder and staggered away from his opponent. The TRIO goon adroitly kicked the Phoenix fighter's legs out from under him, and McCarter crashed on his back.

He saw the Japanese hit man raise the sickle end and quickly rolled to the side as the killer hurled his blade. The crescent knife struck wood near McCarter's left shoulder, missing his neck by scant inches. The Briton's feet snaked out to snare his opponent's closest leg.

It was an old SAS jijitsu trick. McCarter hooked one boot behind the TRIO man's ankle and stamped the other against his knee. The killer yelled in anger and pain as he was thrown to the deck. McCarter quickly rushed his opponent while the man was still trying to adjust his *kusarigama* for a counterattack.

McCarter pounced on the bastard and rammed his fist between the man's eyes. The Briton followed through with a karate chop across the bridge of the bloke's nose and then drove a heel of the palm stroke under the killer's nostrils. The broken shards of cartilage and bone was shoved up into the goon's brain, killing him in the blink of an eye.

Calvin James cleared the top of the ladder, a .357 Colt Python in his fist. He was alarmed when he saw McCarter on the deck until he realized the Briton was unharmed.

"Come on, man," James told him. "Get up. We got work to do."

"Silly sod," McCarter growled in reply as he located his fallen Ingram and checked it for possible damage.

McCarter and James moved aside as the rest of the Phoenix commandos joined them aboard the decks of *El Astro*. The Briton and the black man turned toward the bow of the yacht, while Katz, Encizo and Manning hurried to the vessel's starboard quarter.

Yakov Katzenelenbogen cautiously rounded the corner of the afterbulkhead. To the Israeli's right was a narrow stairway leading up to the bridge. Several feet beyond were the companionway steps going below. No sooner had Katz digested this information than the companionway entrance was filled with a pair of TRIO gunmen looking for blood.

Upon sighting the Israeli, the first of the killers snarled in rage and swung his Nambu automatic around to cut Katz down. The former Mossad agent had other ideas and triggered his Uzi to stitch a line of 9mm slugs across the *yakuza* gunsel's chest and right hand.

The Japanese hood screamed and tried to gun down the heavyset Caucasian responsible for his dire condition. His trigger finger refused to cooperate, the reason for this digital mutiny being that the finger no longer existed.

With blood spurting from the stump where his finger had been, the assassin's Nambu slipped from his grasp to the deck of the yacht. The killer shivered and felt life drain from his body, but he didn't go down. Drawing his last breath with bullet-punctured lungs, the dying man surged forward.

His corpse fell against Katz, deflecting the Uzi toward the deck. The second TRIO assassin aimed his Chinese Tokarov and prepared to open fire. Rafael Encizo's MP-5 snarled before the gunman could squeeze the trigger. Two hollowpoint parabellums gouged through the front of the TRIO hood's face, knifing through brain matter to blast open the back of his skull.

Gary Manning left the Hechler&Koch G-3 rifle with Mahmud in the catamaran before scaling the ladder to *El Astro*. The Canadian drew his Eagle .357 Magnum as he moved across the deck toward a small row of steps leading to the bridge. Manning approached stealthily, aware that the bridge would be a perfect nest for TRIO gunmen to hide in. The fact that no attack had come from that direction thus far meant nothing. The trick was to get the enemy to show their hand before he had to show his.

The Canadian moved to the cover of a pair of lifeboats mounted on a wooden rack. He shuffled behind the survival gear to discover a Mongol bullyboy was waiting for him. The TRIO thug lashed out with a club, striking the Magnum from Manning's hand. The Mongol quickly jabbed the end of his stick into the Canadian's belly.

Manning doubled up as his opponent raised the club, about to bash in the Phoenix warrior's brains.

At that moment, Manning lunged forward and caught the killer's wrist, holding back the cudgel. The Canadian rammed a knee between the Mongol's legs and the TRIO flunky groaned in agony as Manning seized his opponent and turned sharply.

He adroitly hauled the killer over a hip in a simple judo throw. The Mongol smacked the deck and Manning stomped a boot under his opponent's chin, driving the edge of his foot into the bastard's throat. The blow crushed the TRIO hood's windpipe, killing him. The Canadian retrieved his Eagle pistol and examined the dead man.

Manning gathered up the Mongol's corpse and easily hauled the body across a brawny shoulder. As Katz and Encizo moved toward the companionway leading below, Manning hefted his burden into a fireman's carry and climbed the steps to the bridge.

"Your men seem to be getting the shit kicked out of them, Matsuno!" Ferris observed as enemy gunfire appeared to saturate *El Astro* from all sides. The ONI renegade was crouched behind a partition of solid oak, his eyes darting about fearfully like an animal caught in a cage.

Directly across from Ferris was the narrow companionway leading from the bridge. Shots erupted just beyond his field of vision. Ferris was not about to raise his head to get a better look. He did not have to see what a mess they were in. Ferris shook his head with disgust and caressed the barrel of his magnaported S&W M-29 revolver. Right now, the big .44 Magnum was the only friend he had. The only thing he could believe in.

Sadatoshi Matsuno gripped the hilt of his *katana* and shuddered. The American traitor was correct. The TRIO warriors aboard *El Astro* were proving no match for the fury of the five mysterious foreigners Matsuno had hoped the gods would destroy. Those five demons had crushed TRIO's well-orchestrated scheme to seize and resell the *Bruja del Mar*'s precious cargo.

Matsuno scowled, his sensitive hearing picking up the creaking of footsteps on wood.

"The stairs!" Matsuno warned.

Ferris jerked at the sound of Matsuno's voice and fired his M-29 at the shadowy figure that appeared at the head of the stairs.

CALVIN JAMES and David McCarter reached the foredeck as four armed TRIO killers scrambled out through a hatch and onto the bow of the yacht.

"Liu-shen!" the first assassin to spot the Phoenix duo cried, his call of alarm drowning in his throat as a couple of M-10 missiles sliced his world of corruption-by-the-numbers to a big fat zero. His legs gave way at the knees and he collapsed over the bodies of other TRIO low life who had already been killed during the fierce battle.

One TRIO gunsel shrieked as an avalanche of lead caved in his chest and threw him stumbling against the cretin beside him. The second killer regained his balance only to lose it and everything else with a between-the-eyes slug from James's Colt. Both losers fell upon the rapidly growing piles of TRIO dead.

The fourth assassin bowed out forever by blasting a hole in the clouds with his Thompson M-1 submachine gun; his faulty aim directly related to the overwhelming amount of Ingram lead lodged in the left ventricle of his *sushi*-loving heart. The Thompson clattered to the deck as its Japanese owner did the same.

"So much for this bunch," Calvin James said, crossing with McCarter to the bow of the yacht. "Looks like their final act."

"Right," the Briton agreed. "Curtains."

KATZ AND ENCIZO were two steps down the companionway when the Mongolians opened fire, chewing the steps at the feet of the Phoenix pair to splinters. The Israeli and Cuban scurried topside for cover.

"Sociable bunch," Encizo commented as he reached for an M-26 frag grenade.

"Maybe they have a dress code," Katz wryly suggested as he followed the Cuban's example.

Both men pulled the pins and tossed the grenades down the companionway. The twin explosions rocked the vessel. Screams echoed up from the hold as Katz and Encizo charged down the companionway, weapons blazing. The tidal wave of 9mm rounds ended the suffering of a grenade-maimed Mongol whose right arm and leg had been ripped from their sockets. The other TRIO henchmen were already beyond pain.

FERRIS DESPERATELY TRIGGERED HIS MAGNUM again and again, pumping powerful .44 slugs into the figure on the companionway of the bridge. Jesus Christ, the traitor thought. Why won't this bastard fall? He fired the sixth round and the hammer of his S&W blaster struck an empty chamber.

Gary Manning released the corpse of the TRIO goon he had carried up the companionway and had held erect to draw the fire of the TRIO forces hidden on the bridge. The mangled, bullet-crushed body tumbled down the companionway as Manning removed an AN-MB smoke grenade from his belt. He pulled the safety pin and launched the grenade with an overhand toss into the bridge.

Ferris panicked as the grenade sailed through the entrance to the bridge and began spewing out a thick column of blinding white smoke. While the dense fog filled the bridge, Matsuno stood and pushed open an emergency overhead escape hatch. The Japanese quickly hauled himself through the gap up to the roof. Silently Matsuno lowered the hatch cover into place.

Manning entered the bridge, Eagle pistol in hand. Ferris fumbled with his .44 Magnum, shoving six rounds from a speedloader into the chambers. He snapped the cylinder shut and mopped the back of a hand across his sweaty brow.

"Drop it!" Manning ordered.

Ferris swung his M-29 toward the voice, and Manning fired his Eagle twice. The ONI turncoat screamed and fell into a corner, the .44 sliding across the floor from his trembling body.

Manning strained his eyes to see through the haze of white smoke. He saw the enemy's revolver and kicked it aside. Then he found Ferris. The ONI renegade was bleeding to death from two separate wounds to the stomach. He was trying to staunch the red flow pouring into his lap. He would have had more luck trying to tie a tourniquet around his neck.

"Ferris or Mitchell?" Manning asked.

Ferris blinked through the smoke and raised his tear-drenched eyes. "Mitchell...Mitchell is dead."

"That makes two of you."

Manning fired his Eagle one more time, quickly ending the dying man's pain.

Matsuno flattened his body against the roof as he watched the Canadian descend the companionway to the main deck where the other four members of Phoenix Force were waiting for him.

Matsuno would have given anything at the moment for another weapon besides his honored *katana*. But it was not to be. His karma had denied him the honor of killing the five foes. Instead, Matsuno fixed the faces of each enemy indelibly upon his mind. He withdrew from the edge of the roof. At all costs TRIO must be warned of these most persistent enemies.

Alongside *El Astro* in the smuggler's catamaran, Mahmud caught the stealthy movement of a shadowy figure creeping across the roof of the yacht bridge.

"Stop!" Mahmud yelled, raising the H&K G-3 rifle.

The lone figure atop the bridge rose to an upright position, a long sword flashing in his hand. The TRIO killer was charging toward Mahmud.

Mahmud aimed and fired. The Bajau's target screamed, his *katana* falling from his hands as he clutched at the wound in his side. The TRIO assassin rushed to where the roof ended and slipped over the edge, plunging into the sea between the yacht and the catamaran.

Mahmud lowered the G-3 and looked down at the water. Only bubbles marked the spot where the killer had fallen.

"Are you all right, mate?" McCarter said as he came running to investigate the shooting.

"Fine, thank you," Mahmud said and grinned, staring at *El Astro* as the remaining members of the Phoenix Force team joined McCarter. "The shooting you heard was me taking care of a stray fighter of TRIO that you missed. He tried to attack me. I shot him. He fell into the sea."

"Good show, Mahmud," McCarter said.

Katz turned to McCarter and Calvin James. "What about the remainder of the treasure from the *Bruja del Mar*?"

"Belowdeck," Calvin supplied. "All crated up and ready to go."

"Excellent," Encizo pronounced.

Katz nodded. "We'll radio Subic Bay and have them meet us with an escort. And after that..."

"We head for home," Gary Manning said.

"Bloody right to that!" McCarter agreed. "We're all through here. End of story."

EPILOGUE

Sadatoshi Matsuno dragged his bleeding body upon the sandy shore of Bunabunaan Island. His gunshot wound burned with fire, but Matsuno ignored the hurt. His spirit was too full of *haji*, or shame, to leave room for pain.

TRIO had failed. All of the men under Matsuno's command were dead. The treasure TRIO would have auctioned was no longer TRIO's to sell. Even Matsuno's *katana* had been stolen from him.

Sadatoshi Matsuno's shame was great. And all because of the five foreigners. One black man. Four white. All enemies of TRIO. Matsuno would never forget their faces. He would always remember.

The day would come when he and TRIO would meet the foreigners again. Matsuno was sure of it. Positive.

Sadatoshi Matsuno did not believe in accidents.

**MORE GREAT ACTION
COMING SOON**

PHOENIX FORCE

#20 Tooth and Claw

PHOENIX ON FIRE

The Russians assemble a proactive strike force
consisting of their best KGB operatives, Morkrie
Dela assassins and Special Forces commandos.
Launched from an American base, the crack hit
squad has their radar locked on the Phoenix Force
freedom fighters. While the Force fights for
survival, the Soviets prepare to carry out their
single but deadly order:
Terminate with extreme prejudice.

Available soon wherever paperbacks are sold or through Gold Eagle Reader
Service. In U.S.A.: 2504 W. Southern Avenue, Tempe, Arizona 85282. In Canada:
P.O. Box 2800, Postal Station A, 5170 Yonge Street, Willowdale, Ont. M2N 6J3.

Enter the
'Gear Up For Adventure Sweepstakes'
You May Win a 1986 AMC Jeep® CJ
Off-road adventure — Only in a Jeep.®

OFFICIAL RULES
No Purchase Necessary

1) To enter print your name, address and zip code on an Official Entry or on a 3" x 5" piece of paper. Enter as often as you choose but only one entry allowed to each envelope. Entries must be postmarked by January 17, 1986 and received by January 31, 1986. Mail entries first class. In Canada to Gold Eagle Gear Up For Adventure Sweepstakes, Suite 233, 238 Davenport Rd., Toronto, Ontario M5R 1J6. In the United States to Gold Eagle® Gear Up For Adventure Sweepstakes, P.O. Box 797, Cooper Station, New York, New York 10276. Sponsor is not responsible for lost, late, misdirected or illegible entries or mail. Sweepstakes open to residents 18 years or older at entry of Canada (except Quebec) and the United States. Employees and their immediate families and household of Harlequin Enterprises Limited, their affiliated companies, retailers, distributors, printers, agencies, American Motors Corporation and RONALD SMILEY INC. are excluded. This offer appears in Gold Eagle publications during the sweepstakes program and at participating retailers. All Federal, Provincial, State and local laws apply. Void in Quebec and where prohibited or restricted by law.

2) First Prize awarded is a 1986 Jeep CJ with black soft top and standard equipment. Color and delivery date subject to availability. Vehicle license, driver license, insurance, title fees and taxes are the winner's responsibility. The approximate retail value is $8,500 U.S./$10,625 Canadian. 10 Second Prizes awarded of a Sports Binocular. The approximate retail value is $90 U.S./$112.50 Canadian. 100 Third Prizes awarded of Gold Eagle Sunglasses. The approximate retail value is $6.95 U.S./$8.65 Canadian. No substitution, duplication or cash redemption of prizes. First Prize distributed from U.S.A.

3) Winners will be selected in random drawings from all valid entries under the supervision of RONALD SMILEY INC. an independent judging organization whose decisions are final. Odds of winning depend on total number of entries received. First prize winner will be notified by certified mail and must return an Affidavit of Compliance within 10 days of notification: Winner residents of Canada must correctly answer a time-related arithmetical skill-testing question. Affidavits and prizes that are refused or undeliverable will result in alternate winners randomly drawn. The First Prize winner may be asked for the use of their name and photo without additional compensation. Income tax and other taxes are prize winners' responsibility.

4) For a major prize winner list, Canadian residents send a stamped, self addressed envelope to Gold Eagle Winner Headquarters, Suite 157, 238 Davenport Road, Toronto, Ontario M5R 1J6. United States residents send a stamped, self-addressed envelope to Gold Eagle Winner Headquarters, P.O. Box 182, Bowling Green Station, New York, NY 10274. Winner list requests may not include entries and must be received by January 31, 1986 for response.

A division of
WORLDWIDE LIBRARY®

GOLD EAGLE

THE MAGAZINE OF ACTION ADVENTURE

Get the *inside track* on the *guts* of the action adventure scene. Automag is North America's *only* magazine of this type, filled with action-packed news and updates on everything from new books to weapon reviews.

**Try one for FREE,
just by sending a stamped,
self-addressed envelope to:**

Automag Offer
Gold Eagle Reader Service
2504 W. Southern Ave.
Tempe, AZ 85282

**No risk—no obligation.
See what you've been missing!**

AMI/R

NAME (PLEASE PRINT)

ADDRESS   APT. NO.

CITY   STATE/PROV.   ZIP/POSTAL CODE

Offer not valid to current subscribers.

GET THE
NEW WAR BOOK
AND MACK BOLAN
BUMPER STICKER FREE!
Mail this coupon today!

FREE! THE NEW WAR BOOK AND MACK BOLAN BUMPER STICKER
when you join our home subscription plan.

Gold Eagle Reader Service, a division of Worldwide Library
In U.S.A.: 2504 W. Southern Avenue, Tempe, Arizona 85282
In Canada: P.O. Box 2800, Postal Station A, 5170 Yonge Street, Willowdale, Ont. M2N 6J3

YES, rush me The New War Book and Mack Bolan bumper sticker FREE, and, under separate cover, my first six Gold Eagle novels. These first six books are mine to examine free for 10 days. If I am not entirely satisfied with these books, I will return them within 10 days and owe nothing. If I decide to keep these novels, I will pay just $1.95 per book (total $11.70). I will then receive the six Gold Eagle novels every other month, and will be billed the same low price of $11.70 per shipment. I understand that each shipment will contain two Mack Bolan novels, and one each from the Able Team, Phoenix Force, SOBs and Track libraries. There are no shipping and handling or any other hidden charges. I may cancel this arrangement at any time, and The New War Book and bumper sticker are mine to keep as gifts, even if I do not buy any additional books.

IMPORTANT BONUS: If I continue to be an active subscriber to Gold Eagle Reader Service, you will send me FREE, with every shipment, the AUTOMAG newsletter as a FREE BONUS!

Name	(please print)
Address	Apt. No.
City	State/Province	Zip/Postal Code
Signature	(If under 18, parent or guardian must sign.)

This offer limited to one order per household. We reserve the right to exercise discretion in granting membership. If price changes are necessary you will be notified.

166-BPM-BPGE   AA-SUB-1R